J. MERRITT LYONS

Distract Me til I…

Published by:

The Running Tap
therunningtap.com

DISTRACT ME TIL I...

About the Author

J. Merritt Lyons was educated at the University of Illinois in Urbana-Champaign and the University of Warwick in Coventry, England. *Distract Me til I...* is J Merritt's first published work of short stories. He lives in Naperville, IL with his wife and son.

DISTRACT ME TIL I...

Thank you Khalilah and Matt

DISTRACT ME TIL I...

Stories

Dance with Me

Curiosity

Here and There

Estrangement

Gun in My Hand

The Seed

King

Lost

Streets

Three Sounds

The Color of Love and Batteries

The Track

What's Crazy

Vanishing Faces

One Hour before the Veil of Vesuvius

Dull Pressure Strangulation

Suburban Samaritan

Hope

Kill My Dealer

The Red Neon Sign

Chicago

Distract Me til I Die

DISTRACT ME TIL I…

Dance with Me

Dance with me, she said.
Okay, I said.

Do you like it?
No.
Keep dancing, you will.
Okay.

And I did.

Curiosity

The road was black and straight and hot and flat. The day was clear beneath the blue sky and sparsely scattered white clouds. I did not know exactly where I was going. I had no tangible destination. I could not slow down, exit and return to where I had been. That much was certain. I was in my 29th year and I'd decided to fold the hand I'd been dealt, to abandon what I'd become and drive west. Quite cliché yes, but motion beat sedentary decay.

I was cruising amidst the flat land of middle America when I decided to move my foot from accelerator to break and exit the forward race of the fast road. I slowed the roll of my car and entered the lazy calm of a small town not yet captured by the big mart and the chain food. I suddenly craved a cold beer, a hot bite, a brand new view. Something different. A slap across the worn face of my perspective.

I settled on a modest café with modest décor and modest prices. I'd tell you the name of this café but then you'd go looking for it, and I have no wish to inspire such action, action taken by the desperate reader who gets high off the true tale of another and would like nothing more than to rub his lonesome erection on the artifact of an identity that was never meant to be his, to be known by him, to be wanted by him, an identity long gone and dead.

I entered the darkness of the café interior and immediately requested a table outside. The waitress was fat, her hair not styled pretty, her demeanor kind. It was a warm summer month, a mid-week afternoon. I took a seat on the patio, several tables apart from a light brown skinned girl. She was sitting alone amongst the empty square tables and stiff metal chairs. Her head was low, the pencil in her hand moving.

I sipped a cold beer and observed the landscape around me. The sun was blazing from the South, illuminating the open land of the Midwest plains. A farmhouse stood strong in the distance with children playing and a dog barking. Such a contrast to the cluttered charge of the big city.

Returning my gaze to the brown skinned girl in the café, I became increasingly curious with the mystery that was her. I admired the intensity of her eyes as they followed the words she penned. That a girl with so much beauty would be dining in such isolation and engaged in an activity that captured her with such seriousness fascinated me. The revolving door of my imagination pondered what thoughts she was suffering that incited such words and fueled such intensity.

She was a very pretty girl. Big eyes, brown skin, dark curly hair, nice breasts filling a small, rather plain white t-shirt, slender legs fitted nicely inside a pair of dark jeans, one cute bare brown foot rubbing the other, sandals discarded to the side.

How hard she pressed that pencil, how cemented the expression on her face was. Some thought or memory appeared to have a tight grip upon her mood and it wasn't a comforting one. It's a magical thing how even a pretty girl still looks pretty, no matter how high or low her mood becomes. It is only the face of the beauty that alters. How did ugly people manage, I wondered.

I watched this girl- this serious, somewhat sad but pretty girl. I watched her with pity. With sedated lust. With calm. Then with desperation. Then a forced detachment. Then a curious obsession. How I felt and what I thought changed as quickly as the shadows of a tree on a windy day. I tilted the glass to my lips and couldn't help but smile as I enjoyed the refreshing effects of a cold dark beer. I wrote on a napkin: *such liberation to be released from the nonsense of my self-bondage.*

On this warm day at a café in the small middle of a massive America, I cared not how this very pretty and serious girl would perceive me. I was simply curious. That was all. Caring was a thing of the past. Emotional investment had been displaced with curious detachment. But then I did care, so I ordered another beer. I've always admired drunk people. They appear more free.

A few swigs later my affection for the simple landscape surrounding me began to rise. I could see myself spending more time here. Perhaps finding a job and a cheap place to live. Making some friends, finding a temporary lover and then heading on my way, free from too much commitment, liberated from the dangers of caring. Another couple swigs and my growing curiosity swam in synch with a growing courage. I wanted to know this girl, her truth beyond my bias imagination.

***

In recent weeks I had quit my job, broke up with a girlfriend who had emotionally split months prior, forgiven my father's tombstone, given my collection of paintings to friends and friends of friends, cashed out my possessions for a purse of $4,237 and visited my childhood church to determine if there was anything there for me. There wasn't.

My next decision: travel west. Get in the car and drive. Just fucking go.

15 hrs later I sat in this small town café wondering if a somewhat sad but pretty girl would talk to me. Did I care or was I curious? I finished my beer and determined I was simply curious. I ordered another beer.

Cold beer in hand, I decided to meet this pretty girl with brown skin and cute feet. I walked to her table and sat across from her. She looked up, not surprised but rather annoyed.   My courage blinked. My purpose abandoned me. My expression was stuck in some land of in between.

"Do you get off on acting all fucking weird or something?" She asked.

"No," I said. "I—

"Oh I suppose now you have some clever pickup line," she said, "maybe something about how my beauty rendered you speechless?"

I laughed a somewhat nervous laugh. She did not smile.

"Sorry," I said. "I had some reason to come over here and I can't pinpoint it all of a sudden. To be perfectly honest it was rooted in some fascination with you." She leaned back, crossed her arms, a slight concern spreading across her face. "Nothing weird or anything," I smiled unconvincingly. "Curious is probably a better word. A pretty girl so intensely writing at a café by herself on a midweek afternoon -- that's intriguing to me."

12

"I'm not sure what is so intriguing about that. You've never seen a girl sitting by herself writing before?"

"What are you writing?" I asked. "Looks like a letter of some sort."

"Why is that any of your business?"

"Curious," I said, more at ease.

"Are you always this rude?"

"I'm not rude," I laughed gently. "I would be rude if you told me to get lost and I stayed anyway. People abuse the word rude. Meeting people is what it's all about. There's no greater energy to be tapped into than human interaction, especially two strangers who share a mutual curiosity."

"I think you need to lay off the sauce. Your confidence is becoming inebriated."

"You are curious and I am curious, so that would be sharing a mutual curiosity, would it not?"

"How on God's green earth have you concluded that I am curious about you?" She turned to the waitress. "Hey Cindy, can you get this drunk some water?" The waitress smiled and nodded.

"No need Cindy," I laughed. "The beer is just fine." I put my beer on the table. "Anyway, to answer your question – you do appear curious. When people aren't curious, they move on because they are bored or uninterested or feel like they are wasting their time. It is curiosity that gives a thing or person possibility in the mind. That is why you haven't told me to fuck off."

She rolled her big brown eyes and sighed. "You sound like you've got it all figured out. Not sure what the point of having it all figured out is, but you apparently do."

"Not really. You're good looking so naturally I am curious. You don't see me all that curious about Cindy now do you? She's not pretty so I don't see the benefit in chatting her up."

"Wow, aren't you the typical shallow guy? Cindy may be a helluva lot more interesting than me. You shouldn't allow yourself to be so easily intoxicated by a woman's surface beauty. That's quite weak, not to mention unimpressive." Her demeanor suddenly softened as she said this.

"Yeah, I guess you're right," I said, "At least I'm honest. I get my kicks from attractive women. So what? Physical desire trumps intellectual desire and that does make me a bit of a shallow jerk but I'm not all that different than most people, including women."

"Do you pride yourself on being like everyone else?"

"Not exactly. Okay okay," I relented. "I'm a shallow jerk and that is not all that impressive and I need to work on that. Are you happy?"

"Yes," she said with satisfaction. "I'm glad we had this breakthrough."

I laughed. She smiled. We both looked into the sky. I took a deep breath of the warm summer air and wondered what to say next. Seconds turned to minutes. I glanced at my empty beer glass.

"I can't say I'm all that different," she said, breaking the silence.

"How so?" I asked.

"Well, would I be putting up with this shit if you weren't a cute guy who obviously is not from around here and therefore possesses some bit of mystery?"

"Oh sure you would," I said. "If I were a fat stumpy dude with thinning hair and a goatee I am sure you would be just as curious."

"Yeah right," she smiled.

What a gorgeous girl she was. A perfect caramel colored skin with intricate brown eyes and a natural wide smile. She wasn't without pain though. There was a wariness in her face that her beauty trumped but couldn't hide.

"I'm afraid to say I'm a bit shallow at times myself," she lightly laughed.

14

"Well look at that! We are a match made in heaven. We might as well go get married," I said, strangely serious, sadly hopeful.

She laughed and said: "And in our vows we will state: *until death or fading beauty do we part.*"

"Perfect!" I laughed. She laughed.

"Can I buy you a beer?" I asked. She nodded. Cindy quickly brought us two beers.

"So what brings you to this sunny, insignificant part of America?" She asked.

I bury my nose in my glass, unsure of how to respond. "Breaking free I suppose."

"From what?" she asked.

"Oh Jesus, I don't know. Caring I guess. That word pretty much sums it up."

"What exactly were you caring so much about?" She asked, sipping her beer, eyes on my response.

"Everything really. But it was all centered around a single pursuit. And that pursuit enflamed my caring about everything else."

"What was this single pursuit? Some material pursuit? A big shot businessman or something?"

"No no no, not at all. Quite the opposite. For the last ten or eleven years I had grown increasingly obsessed with realizing the identity of an artist. A *highly revered* artist."

"What kind of art?"

"Painting. You know, like the next Dali or something."

"Dali, hugh? I heard he was a self-absorbed moron," she said.

I laughed weakly. "Well there you go," I said. "I'm glad I quit then."

"Are you any good? *Were* you any good?"

"I don't know and I no longer care. It's pointless to care. I'd rather just be. It's like thinking vs. acting. Or dreaming vs. living-"

"Or imagining vs. experiencing?"

"Exactly!" I said. "It was all so pointless and motionless. A path to paranoia and insecurity."

"And perpetual discontent I am sure," she said.

"Yes. Brief highs never sustained. Too much caring, as I've said." I shook my body. "I shudder at the thought of caring that much." A rising energy began to uplift me as I wondered if she was leading a parallel path to mine and this encounter was some sort of strange fate.
"You seem to really understand this shit I am going through," I said.

"Yeah," she sighed, looking downward and picking at her torn jeans. "I have a past as well. Maybe once you get beyond this little confessional of yours, we can get to me." She said with a playful smile.

"Shit, I'm sorry. I *am* being a little self-absorbed, aren't I? Let's talk about you."

"Let's not," she laughed, genuinely amused by this suggestion.

"What's your name?" I asked.

She ignored my question and said, "I get what you have been saying to me but I think you are being a little dramatic with the whole thing. Which is understandable considering you're an artist."

"*Was* an artist."

"No, you *are* an artist," she said. "There is no *was* with that sort of thing. Don't be so naive."

"Geez, you really tell it how it is, hugh?"

"Why wouldn't I?" She asked rhetorically. "Anyway, I think I know what your problem is and it has nothing to do with your actually painting. It has to do with *why* you were painting." She pushed her hair behind her ears and leaned forward in her chair. "Why did you paint anyway?

"I enjoyed it, I guess."

"You enjoyed what?" She asked.

The stiff metal chairs were suddenly very uncomfortable and I shifted for a better position. I shrugged in response to this pretty girl's question. She continued leaning forward, waiting for a response.

I sipped my beer and said, "Creating something. Moving images in my mind to images on canvas."

"At what point did the simple act of creating no longer make you happy?" She asked, quite serious.

"Damn, I feel like I'm in therapy," I laughed weakly.

She just stared at me, waiting for an answer, her expression intense, her beauty radiant.

"I don't know. I-"

"Let me answer this one for you," she said. "Your expectations changed. You said it yourself – you wanted to be *revered*. Shit, not just revered, but *highly* revered. Remember telling me that?"

"Yes," I submitted.

"Okay, what exactly does that *mean* anyway? Being revered is nothing you can control. That is putting the validation of your own happiness in the hands of some arbitrary collection of *others*. That's just fucking stupid. Be more authentic with your art. Do it for the love of it. If you create something you love, then fuck reverence."

I sat stunned. Defeated. Exposed. Feeling somewhat pathetic but slightly hopeful.

"Sorry," she said, breaking a long silence. "That probably came off harsh. I've just lost patience lately with everyone's obsession with validation. Including my own."

"What sort of validation are you seeking?" I asked, overwhelmingly curious.

"Enough about me," she smiled uncomfortably. "I've decided to no longer fight the validation fight. And my solution is not a courageous one. *Yours* can be. And maybe we were meant to meet so I could deliver that message to you. Something in my heart tells me that you do have something special. So don't squander it with some goddamned obsession with validation."

The cliché *love at first sight* kept pulsing through my veins. This beautiful brown girl from the café was eliciting something wild within. "Thank you," I said with weak voice and strong heart.

She smiled and a lone tear rolled down her soft cheek. She didn't wipe it. Her mind had gone to a distant place, her eyes unfocused on the empty plains in the distance. The lonely tear dripped from chin to paper. The paper she had been writing on with such intensity just moments before I sat down.

"Are you okay?" I asked, suddenly concerned with a lover's heart.

Breaking from her drift and wiping the wetness from her face, she smiled. "Allergies…that's all," she said.

"So what are you writing?" I asked, unwilling to abandon my intensifying curiosity.

"Can't tell you, but I admire your curiosity," she smiled.

"Mysterious. I like that. Makes me more curious," I said.

"More curious. Right. Not more caring. You could care less what I am writing. You are just curious," she said - half serious, half joking. I couldn't tell which half meant more.

"That's it, baby," I said with forced detachment. "You've got me figured out."

18

She began putting her things in her bag. Taking a deep breath, she then looked me in the eyes and smiled.

"So what's your name anyway?" I asked with a slight pleading.

"Listen," she said, ignoring my question once more. "I was about to do something this afternoon, but I can put it off until tomorrow. Why don't we go somewhere where we can satisfy both our curiosities?"

I asked her for her name once more as we exited the cafe but she ignored the question. In less than ten minutes we had checked into a motel down the street. Three minutes after that she was unzipping my pants and gripping the head of my erection. She pushed me gently on the bed and her lips met the tip of my penis with a gentle kiss as her hands softly held and caressed me . My hand ran through her dark hair, her scent entering me in waves, each wave intensifying the severity of my erection. She stood up and lifted my shirt off, kissed my chest, unzipped her jeans and pulled them down far enough to expose her white underwear. With my erection in her hand she massaged herself softly. I moved closer and she pulled the white cotton aside and teased me gently. I lifted her shirt up, pulled her bra down and began massaging and kissing and licking her perfect brown breasts. "Squeeze my ass," she whispered. And I did. "Pull my panties down," she whispered. And I did. "Spank me gently," she whispered. And I did. "Harder than that." And I did. She had me partially inside her and asked if I "wanted to". Yes, I told her. You do, she asked. Yes I do, baby. You sure? she asked. Yes, I moaned. She laid me on the hotel bed and pulled my pants fully from my naked legs. She took off her shirt and bra, stepped out of her jeans and panties, and there we were. Her, the pretty girl from the café with no name. Me, the new and improved, the liberated and careless. With my erection in her hand she snaked her way up my naked body. She asked me if I was still curious. I laughed. She laughed. She climbed on top of me and with a slow and methodical grind, took control, her body so perfect, her smell like a drug, her face in the moment, her flesh so warm, so wet, so tight. I noticed she had a black birthmark on the left side of her waist in the shape of a half moon. I gripped this half-moon and in a unified motion with this pretty girl from the café, we made love hard and fast, harder and faster…

***

I asked her if I could see her the next day. She said no, that she had to do that thing she was going to today. I asked her what about the day after. She told me she wouldn't be around, but it was okay, it was cool, as long as I maintained my philosophy of curiosity over caring, it shouldn't matter if I see her again or not. I could only nod without a smile. I suddenly feared wanting her the way I did.

I took a quick shower, hurried by the fear that this pretty girl wouldn't be there when I finished. When I opened the bathroom door I found her with pen to paper, contributing further words to that letter she was writing. She tossed the pen to the side and quickly folded the letter into a small square and slid it into the pocket of her tight jeans. She grabbed her purse and headed towards the door. Turning back as she unlatched the lock and twisted the doorknob, she pushed out an awkward smile and said "goodbye".

"You never told me your name," I said, becoming increasingly concerned by the very real possibility I may never see her again.

"It's not important," she said as she exited. "There are more valuable things than names to be curious about."

I had no response. None that I could express.

"The letter," I gasped loudly just before she shut the motel door. "What about the letter?" I asked.

"What about it?" She asked, sticking her head back in the room, her expression less happy, more strained.

"At least tell me what you were writing," I pleaded with less calm, less cool.

"Here," she said as she threw the folded letter to the floor. "You can read it. Feed your curiosity." She was not smiling as she disappeared into the warm summer day.

Just like that she was gone. I was alone.

Weakened by the drug of desire, I sat on the edge of the bed and for the first time noticed how depressing and dark the hotel room was. The wallpaper was a hideous faded brown print. The dark brown carpeting was hard and flat like concrete. The curtains matched the walls and were thick and drawn tight, eliminating all natural light. Only one of the three lamps actually worked, with its flickering bulb dimming towards a silent death.

I watched the letter on the floor and my disdain for what it represented grew. I had lost my cool. I had wanted too much. Cared too recklessly.

The thought of tracking her down and wildly confessing my love, perhaps expressing some fanatical belief in fate, this thought begged me to burst from the motel room with a wild sort of movie-like obsession. But I couldn't. Wanting anything with such intensity is dangerous and I knew from experience how such wanting never delivers the fantasy we so desperately fabricate and foolishly believe.

So I sat and stared at the stillness of that folded white piece of paper and forced myself to believe I really didn't give a shit what the words she penned on that paper read. I did some pushups, some sit-ups. I turned on the TV, flicked through the cycle of channels three or four times and turned it off. I smelled the sheets for her scent and enjoyed the stiffness of a bittersweet erection.

I replayed our time together over and over again, scanning each recollection for signs that she felt as strongly about me as I did her. I interpreted and reinterpreted and continued to reinterpret her final words and final expressions, a different conclusion resulting each time. Why leave the letter? Why did she look sad when she left? Was she sad? Was it regret for coming or going? Were there signals that I missed and that she so desperately wanted me to receive and then act on in a way that kept her in my arms beneath the sheets, our warm bodies touching? I wondered if she would be as good as it got. If maybe I'd go on traveling west for the next ten years but never feel as good as she made me feel in this hotel room.

I needed to get out. To continue driving west. To have a nice dinner, some strong drinks, some new company in a new place. I needed to make this place a distant memory, the kind of memory I look fondly upon with the emotional detachment time and space provide. I decided to stay the night instead.

The letter remained on the floor as I exited the hotel room and entered the fading late afternoon in search of some fresh air, the lunch I never ordered and some hopeful maybes.

After a large hamburger and several bi-polar drinks, I returned to the flickering brown dying décor of my hotel room. Slightly drunk, I lifted the letter from the floor and began to unfold it. But I couldn't continue. I couldn't read her letter, something so private, something constructed with such intensity and focus. Instead I masturbated to her scent now gone.

I went to bed content with the sedated decision that I would return to the café tomorrow with the letter unread and return it to her. And if she wasn't there I would ask Cindy's help in tracking her down.

When I woke in the morning, the return of sobriety killed resolution and gave birth to conflict. I decided I would get in my car and continue my westward pursuit. But I failed to act and returned to the café instead.

***

It was 11AM when I arrived to the café. It was as empty as the day before. I sat alone on the patio with a cold beer. Her letter was tucked into the pocket of my jeans.

At 11:30 I had only drank half of my beer. Its consumption held no appeal. The   loosened mind that alcohol delivers was not what I presently desired.

The clock reached 12:00 and I remained alone with half a warm beer.

At 12:30 I pulled the letter from my pocket and laid it on the table she had sat at the day before. I was in love with that chair, that table, that concrete floor her beautiful brown feet had touched.

Cindy approached me and asked if I was okay and I said I wasn't sure. I asked her to make sure the girl that sat here yesterday received this letter.

"You mean Victoria," she said.

"What a beautiful name," I said. "Yes, please make sure Victoria gets this. It is hers. Please let her know I never read it."

"Okay. Do you want to give it to her yourself?"

"What do you mean?" I asked.

"I can tell you where she lives. It's not that far from here."

I considered this briefly. Maybe I could have a few beers and stop by with a detached smile.

"No, that's okay," I finally said. "That wouldn't be cool. Just make sure she gets this and let her know I never read it."

Cindy was confused as she took the letter. "Will do," she smiled kindly. I suddenly felt bad for my shallowness as I exited the café.

The day was clear and blue and sunny, but I felt like that hotel room after she left: dark and faded and flickering.
I climbed into my warm car and drove slowly away. Sitting at a stoplight, I debated whether to go back East or head on West.

"Fuck it," I smiled with both strain and relief.

I pulled a joint from my glove box, slid it into my mouth, struck a match, heard the voices of burn, watched the reflections of flame, and headed South with smoke burning my eyes.

Here and There

Child: Why are such large TV's with crystal clear images so popular?

Father: Because we want our fantasies to be as real as possible. We want to feel like we are there.

Child: What's wrong with here?

Estrangement

She slides her cheek across mine and my estrangement from happiness suddenly ceases.

Then I wake to the scream of my alarm clock and my old friend misery suddenly returns. Such is my life, I suppose. Usually depressing and never much laughter. Some in between land of waiting, remembering and imagining, with not a whole lot of that thing called......*progress*.

Goddamn I need to move to another landscape in life. Something different from the same old cereal, the same old *needing*, the same old spin of a revolver with not a single bullet but pretending there is.

I think I'll kill someone today. Someone random. Throw on a black trench coat, some Desert Storm style camouflage pants, hit up a public domain and open fire. Naaaah, that's become such a cliché. So boring. So idiotic. I hate those misguided assholes who pull shit like that. I don't want to be hated. I want to be loved. Adored.

I could find some drugs and a broken human of a hooker and actually care about her tales of a father in prison and a mother plagued by herpes and heroin before I lay her down and pretend she is someone I love. Or hate. Whichever works. Naaah, that would make me the pathetic sort. I don't want to be viewed as *that* guy.

I could always begin a passionate pursuit of a *meaningful* existence...but haven't I done that at least a hundred times before? The answer is a definitive and jaded Yes. What is meaningful anyway?

"Why are you always so fucking reflective on life? Why are you so fucking stuck in your own head?" Shelly asks. Shelly is my skinny companion with heavy acne. I have known her for weeks not years. She rides a vintage red bicycle with a big soft seat.

"Do you think you could use *fuck* one more time in your interrogation of me?" I ask.

"Maybe if I got fucked I wouldn't say fuck so much," Shelly winks.

"Don't look at me," I wince.

"Stop avoiding my question," Shelly says between sips of steaming hot honey water.

"Why do you put honey in hot water and drink it?"

"Stop avoiding my question."

"Because that's how my mind works," I say.

"Who are you?" Shelly asks with strange intensity.

"I don't know," I shrug. "Are you Dr Phil?"

"Did you ever?"

"Did I ever what?"

"Know who you were."

"Yes, once. Maybe."

"When?"

"Before."

I don't have to work. I have money. But I do work because I don't ever intend on spending that money. $989,000. It came in three separate checks. Compensation delivered with a wicked price. It's a pointless life in a pointless world we live...

My boss calls me to deliver an ultimatum but he's the guilty type so he never really gets around to it telling me that I am on the verge of getting fired. He doesn't want to let me go. He's concerned with how I am, even more concerned with whether I plan on taking some time off so he can give my sales territory temporarily to someone who'll help him hit his sales plan so he can make his bonus and be loved again by his boss and his boss's boss. I laugh and tell him no way, that I love my job. I love being on the road and managing insurance agents. It is my passion. My calling. My *therapy*. That one gets him every time. *Therapy.*

"You haven't taken a single day...if anyone is due for a day, it's you," he says with a caring tone.

26

"I can't do that to the agents," I say. "They need me."

"I think they probably feel like I do," he says. "They care about you and worry about you."

"Who says that?"

"Who?" He stalls.

"Yeah, who says they care about me and worry about me." My boss stutters for a moment and I hang up. He doesn't call back.

It is Sunday and I decide to go to a random church and cry. It's of the non-denomination sort, whatever that is. The music is corny and the pastor looks like a creep so I leave without crying. I drive around listening to a CD of lullabies and that makes me cry. I cry until I am tired and go home and sleep. I wake up and feel lonely so I drive to Puppies R Us and buy the ugliest, oldest mut to make myself feel good. It sort of works. I name him Duckling after the Ugly Duckling. Then I feel bad for calling my new best friend such an insulting name so I name him Hilarious. I like that word -- it sort of makes me smile every time I say it. *Come here Hilarious.....thadda boy Hilarious...*

I take my new dog for a walk and he pisses on a cute girl's leg and I yell at him: "Hilarious! Stop that Hilarious!" and the cute girl gives me a look of anger and confusion, then walks off shaking her leg. Halfway home I begin laughing hysterically at how funny that actually was. Hilarious has brought me instant joy and I feel better than I have felt in some time.

"Don't you think you should do something with that money? Maybe invest it or something?" My Mom asks.

"Something," I mumble.

"Something what?" Mom asks.

"What?"

"Are you okay?"

"Yes Mom. Me and Hilarious are doing excellent."

"Who?"

"Hilarious."

"Hugh?"

"Hilarious."

"What is hilarious?"

"Who is hilarious and hilarious is my dog."

"You have a dog?"

"Yeah Mom. I got a dog. Why didn't we ever have a dog when I was little? They are great."

"We did have a dog. He died soon after we got him, remember?"

"I've got to go."

"But honey, I-"

I've always sort of liked people and sort of not liked them. Usually the more honest they are, the more I like them. And the more flawed they are, I like them even more. I don't like "polished" people because polish attempts to erase the honest markings of our history, and it is these markings that make us real. This general philosophy applied to all but my wife. I know this now.

I held him in my arms and fell back in love with my wife. I touched his tiny nose with the tip of my finger and recalled with a strange clarity my own innocence and felt perhaps this was the second chance we are sometimes given, a chance to return to that crossroads where we can once again choose to go right and not wrong.

"I love you so much, honey," my wife said with a tired and emotional smile. "We made that. Can you believe it? We made that. He is both of us."

"Amazing," I said with fear.

"Are you okay," she asked.

I kissed my baby boy and held him to my face, his softness loosened my tense expression.

"Never been better," I said.

"God is so good to us," my wife smiled.

But bad things happen, I thought. To everyone.

The batteries in the Papasan swing are dying because the music is slowing and the empty seat is no longer swinging. 4 batteries per 4 hours nonstop. 336 dead batteries scatter the floor. Hilarious starts barking and I lay down to sleep but can't close my eyes so I stare sideways across the room at my wife's left slipper stuck under the couch. So *that's* where it was.

I have an appointment with a therapist today. Appointed by my company at "no charge". I will not go. Instead I will make plans to leave the country and never return. I make lots of plans. Always have.

I've always thought the major events in my life would change me. 21st birthday, 25 birthday, marriage, 30th birthday, birth of a child. Sometimes we slip on the black ice of our wishful thinking...

"I met you on Match.com?"
"Yes, last night."
"How old are you?"
"19."
"Christ."
"Is that a problem?"
"Are you sexy?"
"Yes."
"Then no, it's not a problem."
"Can I see you?"
"I'm getting hard just talking to you."
"Me too."
"You are getting hard? How is that so?"
"My nipples. I'm also getting wet."
"Oh, okay. Well, do you have a drivers license? Can you meet me at a hotel?"
"Yes, I'm 19, not 15."
"Okay. The Motel 6 off the highway at 7."
I hang up and try to masturbate but feel guilty and decide to take a long dark walk along the lake front.

Sitting on the edge of the pier, the water is thick and dark like oil. People die in this water every year. Like clockwork it is on the news.

The drunk out of towner going for a random midnight walk, the drunk friends going for a swim, the gay immigrant eliminated for two counts of being "un-American". They'll say some by accident, others not. Nothing is an accident though…that much I know.

I finish my beer and toss it into the void of the lake. I blink and suddenly see blue binkies floating like little sailboats in the wavy black oil but am sensible enough to know they aren't really there. Just one of those things my mind plants to remind me of past events that may or may not have happened a certain way. It's all a matter of interpretation and some interpret one way while I can't help interpreting every way.

A young girl sits 20 feet from me on the other side of the pier. She doesn't see me or maybe she does and just doesn't care. Maybe she's weeping. I can't tell. She seems cute and when she stands she staggers a little before screaming something about someone missing her and she jumps off the side of the pier into the black oil of the night. Was she real? I wonder. If she was, am I really a strong enough swimmer to dive into the dark black current of night water and save a drunk and suicidal girl? I am doubtful so I retreat up the pier and ponder which country I will travel to and who will take care of Hilarious and will I ever feel a part of this thing called life or is that simply the me of yesterday who will never be again.

"I once dated a girl whose Mom was from Concord," the skinny thirty-something plumber says after I tell him I grew up in Concord.

"Really?" I ask with no real interest as I roll a joint and stare at the muted Teletubbies on my television.

"Yeah, it didn't work out between us though," he says with his hand in my dark stained toilet, maneuvering God knows what. Could my poop really clog a toilet? I don't *think* I put anything else down there.

"She was, oh what's the word? Promiscuous? Yeah I think it's promiscuous. She basically slept around while she was with me. A lot."

I ignore him as I light my joint and watch it burn without inhaling.

"You learn though. I learned a lot from that," he says, his face in the porcelain. "You know she actually fucked four of my best friends?"

I hesitate to smoke my joint on the account of being in the company of an incredibly pathetic sort of person who creeps me out with the tragedy of a life he so readily shares.

"Yeah, I mean that's what really burns me," he continues. "I thought they were my boys. And they go a screw my girl. I mean she totally had issues. But damn, they were my boys. That's life though. I really learned a lesson." He jerks his hand from the toilet and seems baffled by the number of binkies he is holding. All sorts. Large, small, red, purple, white.

"How long ago was this?" I ask, eager to return to the tragic trajectory of his pathetic life and away from mine.

"15 years," he says, tossing the binkies to the side, no longer contemplating questions like why or how or when.

"Jesus Christ," I say, choking on smoke. "That's a long time ago."

"It was high school. But whatever. Makes me stronger, you know." He rubs his finger on the ring of the toilet, his face calmly sad. "But is really does make you paranoid, you know."

No, I don't.

"Did you know my wife is a parole officer?" He asks, changing subjects.

"Really?" I say with disinterest. How the fuck would I know that?

"Yeah, she deals with a lot of fucked up people."

I exhale a cloud of smoke and feel different, a little more eager to engage, despite the company.

"Then I'm sure your wife more than anyone can understand how life fucks people up and sometimes they become someone or do something that they likely couldn't avoid. Circumstances fucked them to some extent," I say with the sort of depth that usually makes people uncomfortable or opinionated.

"No, fuck that," he says with a sad sort of passion. "I believe we all have our own destinies in our hands and we all make choices. It is entirely up to us to make of life what we want."

"So your friends fucking your girl isn't the reason you are a plumber? You chose to be a plumber? This is what you always wanted? This is your dream?"

With another handful of binkies in his hand, the plumber turns red and confused, a shade of hurt spreading fast into a pathetic sort of expression and body language. Like he might poop himself at any moment. He drops the binkies. Tells me I'm a real asshole. I tell him I am sorry, that I was only joking. Real nice joke, he says. And what's with the Goddamn binkies? Are you some sort of sick fuck? he asks. Free will according to you, I say. A choice I made, I say. A logical choice under illogical circumstances, but a choice none-the-less. Now get the fuck out, I say.

Red with furry and self-pity, the plumber takes the hundred dollar bill from my hand and exits my apartment. I finish my joint and lay on my couch, entranced by the muted Teletubbies.

She wasn't handling things well. A series of poor decisions concerned me. Leaving the baby undressed in his bassinet with the house temperature at 60 degrees. Covering his head with the blanket to keep him warm. Laying him on his stomach next to her in bed. Sleeping through his cries. I wasn't there much but noticed these things when I was. It was just too hard to be home. Too much unhappiness. Besides, Tiffany and I were experiencing something special. Something that made me feel incredibly alive. A welcome change from my wife slowly butchering my contentment to death. I needed some joy. A little laughter. A little of that thing called passion.

"He's such a demanding baby," my wife said with dismay, a glass of wine in her hand. "It's like he is just never satisfied. Always wanting to be held and entertained or fed and changed."

"He's a baby," I said as I put on my coat and searched for my keys.

"Easy for you to say," she says with more than a hint of resentment. "I'm the one who has to spend all fucking day in the apartment with him."

"Well shit, you go get the job and I'll stay home. I'm cool with that."

"Fuck you Elliot. You don't even care about what I am going through."

The truth was that I did and I didn't. I would have been more than happy to be a single father taking care of my baby. It was this marriage thing. This mother and wife thing. I was tired of it. I had only grown increasingly more tired of it. I felt like the embodiment of a played out cliché. I even felt disenchanted enough to entertain the possibilities my wife's death would afford. The freedoms and inspirations. A silly and distant imagining, but an imagining none-the-less. It's not like I wished it or would ever contemplate it as an action, it's just that I found myself wondering more often than I cared to admit what life would be like if my wife no longer played a role.

"It's me," I say with the whisper of a marijuana high.

"Who's me?" She asks.

"The guy from Match.com. We talked yesterday."

"Oh yeah," she says. "Sorry, I couldn't make it to the hotel. Just a little fast for me, you know?"

"I didn't go either. But I did see a girl kill herself last night."

"You what?"

"Nothing. Maybe we should start with coffee."

"Okay."

"Tomorrow at 7AM at the Grindhouse."

"Okay."

I want badly what I don't have, what I just got, what I just lost or what I once had. I never particularly care about what I currently have.

"Do you think I'm fat," my wife would ask.

"Yes, among other things," I would blankly and silently not say.

"Well, do you? Why are you just staring at me? You do think I'm fat don't you? You know you could at least try to make me feel good."

"So you want me to lie to you?" I ask.

"So you do think I'm fat?"

"I was kidding."

"No you weren't. You think I'm fat."

And so it went.

At the Grindhouse. She looks 17. Says she's 19. I ask her why she'd meet a 33 year old off the internet. She says I seemed cool and age is ain't nothing but an illusion invented by the close minded and lawyers. I don't bother probing this statement because maybe I get it and maybe I don't. We exchange hesitant surface jargon until the she randomly alters the course of our meaningless dialogue.

"Do you do drugs?"

"Not anymore," I say.

"Not even weed?"

"Maybe."
"What about pills?"
"What kind of pills?"
"Happy pills that make you feel great and love sex."
"It's been a while."
"Since you took Ecstasy?"
"No, since I felt great and loved sex."
"We should totally gobble some down and see what happens."
"And what normally happens?"
"Dunno, we'll probably fuck all day and night."
"Why would I want to do that? I have things to do."
"Oh come on. It'll blow your mind how much fun you have."
"Are you the devil?"
"I don't think so."

I cared for my baby boy for a week. No wife. No job. No distractions. Just him and me. We walked along the lake. We giggled on the floor. We watched Sesame Street and got bored and decided to listen to music and dance. He loved dancing in my arms. Listening to the soothing lyrics and beats and guitars of Bob Marley. To the strange distortions of Radiohead. To the cool sounds of Steely Dan. The way he looked into my eyes and smiled. His perfect contentment and happiness when I bathed him in the tub and rubbed baby lotion on his smooth small body. The smile on my face when he woke me in the middle of the night for a warm bottle of food. His warm cheek against mine, his strong small hands squeezing my fingers. The peaceful beauty in his face when he slept in my arms. My perfect joy. Just my baby boy and me alone for a week in the paradise of now. Then my wife returned and my heart tightened and my mind twisted and I finally returned Tiffani's calls.

When I spoke to Tiffani she was angry I did not spend time with her when my wife was away. I asked her if she was kidding. She said no. That is when I knew I must break off our relationship.

23

Evil is alive and well. We all possess the tools of evil. But we also possess the tools of good. What drives us to pick up which tools? And what happens when we pick up both?

It was summer. We were staying the weekend in the city. My wife, my baby boy and me. I was tight and discontent and then we shared a bottle of champagne. She had half a glass and I the rest. I felt better. Less tense. Less like divorcing my wife.

The following evening I drank too much while my wife and baby slept in the hotel room. I then met Tiffani and we kissed and I returned to the room drunk and electrified by the kiss of a strange girl in a hotel bar who was pretty and kind. My wife was angry and I felt momentarily free so I didn't care. The next morning I masturbated to the memory of that kiss while my wife clothed our baby boy with a frown.

"What's wrong?"

"Nothing"

"I'm not an idiot. Something is wrong."

"Nothing is wrong."

"Whatever."

"Whatever."

The rain is falling and the air is warm. I stand at an intersection in the city and look at my reflection in a storefront window. I am too pale for summer and wonder if I shouldn't do what I have planned to do. Cash one of the checks and hit the globe. That's what I've always wanted to do. Be free. Be alone. Romanticize the earth and the people that inhabit its varieties.

I am high but not high at all. Marijuana has lost its effect on me. No matter how much I smoke.

Lust is a distant feeling that once held sway over me. Maybe it's all the marijuana. Maybe it's the loneliness. Maybe I need to call the 19 yr old and take some of those pills.

I continue to stand at the intersection uncertain as to which direction to walk. None hold any real appeal. I have no destination. It's been forever since I did. Without fantasy and without reality I am stuck in some strange purgatory of existence that renders me immobile. I want nothing. I remember everything. I feel nothing.

A beggar leans against a concrete wall, hidden behind the revelations of his yellow beard. His filthy hot pants grow increasingly damp but he is sheltered from the rain. He is peeing himself. His eyes are drunk and his smile is dead. I always wondered how this happens. Now I know.

Did my discontent destroy? Who's to blame for such a thing? Was she predisposed to such a rapid deterioration? Was I predisposed to such emotional disconnectedness? If he is gone, should I not follow? Why do I seek pleasure through my misery? Could I be the monster they say I am? What do they know that I do not? I loved that boy. I loved that boy with the greatest intensity. More than yourself? Yes, I believe so but who can ever be sure.

"You are taking sleeping pills now?"
"The doctor recommended them," she said.
"Is that safe with the baby?"
"It's fine. I won't sleep through his cries."
"I'm worried."
"Then why don't you stay home for once? Why all the travel? If you're so worried you should be here taking care of your wife and baby. If you are such a great guy. Such a great fucking father."
I spent the next three nights sleeping with Tiffani. Each morning I called home terrified I would be calling home to an unconscious wife and a dead baby. I would be spared such misfortune.

"Do you still love me?"
"Yes."
"Are you sure?"
"Yes."
"Do you love our son?"
"What a stupid fucking question. Of course I do!"
"Why not the same passion when asked about your love for me?"

Tiffani was my age and pretty but age was not going to treat her well. The signs were already there. She really dug me and she was hyper-sexual. But she was pseudo-cool. Tried too hard. Wasn't natural enough with her cool, which nagged me. It's those nagging things that signal to us that the romance will expire sooner than later. She adored me which in retrospect was what I was looking for. Sex and adoration. Analyze it as you may.

"Will you leave her for me?"

"Don't be such a cliché."

"Whatever. It's just a question."

"No. When I leave her I will leave her for me. Marriage is poisonous. And I've already asked you not to get too emotional with this. We are enjoying a period of joy in the timeline of our respective lives. Let's not make it more than it is. Tomorrow we can walk away and remember fondly the energy we shared. If either one of us overstays our welcome then we only begin to tape over this memory of joy with regretful reels of bickering and sadness."

"Whatever."

Fuck you.

Shelly lets me ride her bike and it makes me feel a little strange which I embrace. Her acne seems to be clearing up a little and a trace of prettiness begins to emerge.

"Do you know you are my only friend?" I say.

"I don't even know you."

"You know enough."

"I know your name, that you like cream and sugar in your coffee and that you are fucking depressed a lot. That is hardly knowing a friend."

"Why complicate things with details."

"I suppose."

"Do you want to go have sex somewhere?"

"You don't even want to have sex with me. So no. Even though I would love it."

"Fair enough," I smile.

Shelly hasn't had a fair life. And it couldn't have been her fault. She just isn't attractive and she has strange interests like riding a bicycle and sleeping in parks and befriending bugs that crawl on her in the park. Yet she seems so happy. I wonder if being alienated from society for an entire life isn't really a blessing of sorts. She has learned to cope with this alienation in a fiercely independent way that frees her from the bondage of self-conscious concerns and premeditations.

"Do you care what people think?" I ask.

"What's the point?"

"Do you really mean that or is that just some automatic response that you give to appear aloof and cool?"

"These days I do mean it. I suppose there was a breaking point that led me to really believe it. Not sure when."

"I admire that."

Shelly smiles. Maybe even blushes.

"What is killing you, Elliot? What are the demons that are ripping you apart from the inside?"

I stare at Shelly and want so badly to cry. I haven't felt this emotion for some time. The way her eyes are. The way they have penetrated mine, traveling like a soft lump down my throat and resting on my heart with a gentle sincerity. I want to kiss those eyes. Hug those eyes. Make love to those eyes. I have never experienced eyes like these before.

"I need to go," I say before I cry.

Hilarious' tongue is wetting my face and I wake to the darkness of the late evening. I feed him and fill his water bowl. I walk to the kitchen table and stare at my three checks. I want to burn them but I can't. Maybe if I burn them I will die alone. Maybe if I don't I will cash them and spend them and feel knives of guilt dismembering my insides.

I walk Hilarious under the quarter moon that hovers over the loud city. I contemplate the pier but weird things happen at the pier late at night and I'd rather not enter that dark tragedy of a script on this particular evening. I watch Hilarious and admire how reserved and obedient he is. A loving dog. It's companions like these that make running away or killing oneself more complicated decisions. Maybe Hilarious is my final opportunity at redemption in life. One final chance to live less for self and more for other.

We pass a string of bars where the youth of an intoxicated America battle with their fears and lusts and identities, their greatest weapons being booze and drugs and lies. I hate them and I pity them. What's the point, I ponder. These bars could go up in an inferno and the bodies within turn to ash and what would really change? Friends and relatives and media junkies would feel emotions and fears and perspectives that'd be new and fresh and of actual substance. But how long would that last?

How long until they return to the broken center of their being? What's the point. Let them live or let them die. Let them enjoy the fruits of temporary pleasure. Let them ignore the great demands of selfless love and sacrifice. This is the easier way. We prefer the easier way. Why not. We'll forgive them when they're gone. We always do.

There is such truth in the existence of Hilarious. Is it any wonder that some choose to live their lives among animals and shun society? Am I on my way to a yellow beard and damp pants? Maybe that's why I won't burn those checks. I may not want to be real. Real is lonely and smells like urine.

"I want to try one of those pills."
"I don't have anymore. I did them two nights ago."
"By yourself?"
"No, with a friend."
"A guy?"
"Of course."
"You are the devil."
"Maybe. But one of many and not totally."

We found him together which was odd. Odd to be home together. Odd to be entering the room together. But we both sensed something. I was drunk and preoccupied with my breakup with Tiffani. She was sleeping pill lethargic and in an emotionless haze. But this feeling penetrated both of our broken states. A mutual feeling. A blazing fear. A terror. We woke simultaneously and rushed into his room.

He was too motionless to be sleeping. Too distant to be present. The air in the room too thin and the energy too dark to be anything but the careless presence of death.

I held her as she held him. She kissed him and I kissed her. I stroked the hand that stroked his listless face. She would not let me hold him and that was okay. I loved her more than I had ever loved her before. She needed to know I loved her. I felt that. But it was a day late and a dollar short, as they say. Tomorrow she would be dead and in three days I would be burying both mother and son under the firestorm grief of her hate-filled friends and relatives. Hatred of me. Their villain. Warranted or not, I understood. I understood despite my tear-filled eyes and shaking hands and heart-attack heart. The life inside me was convulsing towards a permanent death, leaving mind and body standing and unwilling to wilt and fall into the grave.

Regret is a tricky mental emotion. It seeks to make simple that which is complicated.

"I'm ready to talk about things."

"Really? You're for real?"

"Yes. Somewhat."

Shelly lays her vintage red bicycle in the grass and flicks her new friend the caterpillar from her arm. Those eyes are traveling through me again. Those damn eyes.

"My baby and my wife both died this year exactly one day apart. And I think it's my fault. I think my selfish discontent caused the death of both. But the odd thing is that I believe this and I don't believe this. I feel this and I don't feel this at all. If that makes any sense."

"I'm going to need more details. What exactly happened?"

"I stopped loving my wife until we found our baby dead. Then I loved her for a day until she died. I loved my baby but I'm not sure I loved him enough to get over the reasons why I didn't love my wife. I struggle remembering why I stopped loving my wife. I had an affair. Her name was Tiffani. She was pretty and sexual and adored me. I think I spent more time with her than my boy, but I'm not sure. I stopped feeling for my wife and I think she felt that deeply and that is why she deteriorated into sedation. And maybe my baby sensed this. Maybe he sensed the madness he was born into and he made a clean break when he could. A drunk and promiscuous father who didn't care about his Mom and a Mom who was so fragile and depressed that she was sinking away before his fresh little eyes. Maybe he just knew. Maybe he'd have just rather remained asleep than wake to a future under the dark cloud of such miserably confused parents. Goddamn. This is what is killing me. But not killing me fast enough. I just don't know. Maybe I caused this all. Maybe not. Maybe I could have saved his Mom and him with a little less demand for my own contentment in life. Maybe I should have. Goddamn Shelly. What am I saying?"

"Come here."

Shelly holds me. She is soft. I close my eyes and feel the wetness on my cheeks. Not a lot but enough. Shelly is so warm and soft and kind. I think I love her. Eyes closed and the honesty of her compassion cradling me. I've never felt such love. I don't want to open my eyes because if I do she won't be beautiful and I won't love her anymore. But I love her now. I love her silent forgiveness of madness. Her acceptance of that which fails.

Gun in My Hand

I've got this gun in my hand. I'm not even sure what kind of gun it is. It belonged to someone I never knew. I bought it from a guy who knew a guy who stole it from some other guy. It doesn't matter, really. All that matters is that I have a gun in my hand. A gun with bullets.

It's a sunny day and the sunshine irritates me. The way it blinds me, the way it reflects off of metallic objects in my house, the way it burns with a fake pleasure. If I could shoot the sun with my gun I would. But I can already see what a futile and dissatisfying exercise it would be; popping off bullets towards such distant and indestructible energy, wondering how far each shot would actually travel, where it may eventually fall.

I stare out my kitchen window at that orange ball of flame and its burning power, a power sometimes too hot, other times not hot at all, just an annoying brightness on a cold day. There was a time when I perceived the sun much differently.

I put on my brown jacket, slide the gun in my pocket and leave my house. I'm not sure where I am going. There are possibilities but no certainties. I have ideas but only quick and sudden bursts of motivation. I see destinations but energy fails to take me the distance. I imagine consequences and conclusions but then imagination alters and I no longer see what I once saw.

My hot breath cools into a white cloud before me. My steps crush the sparkle of the morning's fresh snow. I wonder if I should be nervous. Or angry. Perhaps afraid. Maybe depressed or guilty. Some human emotion that would make me feel real. Some reminder that yes, despite this numbing cloud of self, I am worthy of existing.

I think to myself that perhaps I am suffering a multitude of conflicting feelings. And these feelings are torturing me at varying degrees. And perhaps this intensity renders me without feeling at all.

I was feeling so much for so long. I experienced such a barrage upon my senses. And it had always been those heightened senses that I longed to numb. Thoughts and their emotions relentlessly pursued and controlled me like a hundred thousand flies buzzing within, sometimes burrowed deep within my nerves, traveling viciously to my brain; other times the madness born itself in my brain and spread like spinning blades to the deepest recesses of my nerves.

These thoughts that spawned and fueled emotions alternated between fantastic possibilities and oppressive realities, always returning to the inescapable cruelty of reality.

This winter morning shows me coldness; the ice on the ground, the creatures of summer gone, the chimneys exhaling heavy into the dense gray sky. But I feel nothing. I think everything but feel nothing. I am a shadow, a living creature only halfway to his life expectancy, and I see no reason or hope or fantasy at all. I envision none of the comforting distractions that should spare one from the inevitable cruelties of life, the true nature of things.

I am in a suburb somewhere. The suburb I got married in. I'm not sure why I got married. At the local tavern, on a wobbly bar stool, a few warm whiskeys in my stomach, I used to tell people that my marriage had something to do with fear and love. Many were confused. I told them I feared being alone but that I also loved my wife. "Why do you love her," they would ask. "She's a good woman," I would gush in a fleeting moment of contentment, perhaps even clarity, within the haze of gray smoke, the noise of slurred emphatic chatter, the irritation of a repetitious juke box. "But it was mostly fear," I would eventually say before emptying my glass and spinning it before me. "Fillurup," I would smile with despair.

"What does that mean, exactly?" Many would ask. Apparently they had never heard of anyone marrying out of fear. Love and lust maybe. But fear? I would explain: "Sometimes love alone doesn't inspire marriage. Love alone doesn't satisfy lust for women. Fear doesn't either. But fear avoids loneliness if listened to with enough seriousness. Fear, if potent enough, will convince us that sacrificing independence and suppressing sexual liberation to a point that we find ourselves locked in a bathroom with the lingerie ads from the Sunday paper at the age of 41, is okay. And to a large extent, it is."

Some would laugh knowingly, others mockingly. I didn't give a shit what they thought though. I knew the truth. Somewhere in my heavy gut there was a truth I would rather ignore. It was a reality I had no ability to change. Or maybe I did but I lacked the willingness to accept the likely consequence of failure.

There was a bottom line to all of this. One that has haunted me since my wedding day. One that refused to relinquish its vice grip upon my constant wish for contentment. And it was this:

My wife was no daydream.

Selfless, funny, sociable and smart, yes.

But no daydream.

I remember thinking this the night of our wedding; her body beneath mine, my eyes shut tight, her moans in my ears, my thinking of the young waitress with the tight shirt and perfect breasts who served us dinner earlier that evening in Vegas.

I married when I was 28. It worked for a while. I suppose.

There was a time when I partially convinced myself that what I had was what was truly important. The honesty, the trust, the unconditional love of a woman who cared about me enough to cook me meals, write me poetry, hold me when I was sick; even though she was likely to catch whatever I had, and in many instances did.

But the fantasy possibilities sparked by each day's passing beauty always reminded me how unhappy I was. Desire for beautiful females seemed to increase in gnawing intensity with each spin of the clock. Teased each day by the ceaseless images of beauty on the TV, the erotic romances on the big screen, the high heel clatter of long legs and slender hips down the grocery store isles, the passing perfumes of tan cleavage and tight teenage stomachs while reluctantly strolling through the shopping mall with my wife. I was in a perpetual state of look but don't touch, they may have and I may not, a relentless alternation between happy day dreams and bitter reality.

Did I act on these desires, this insatiable need for the female stimulation? Did I satisfy this sense of worth tied so closely to my

44

ability to conquer, kiss, stroke, lick, penetrate, hold, flaunt a female who's beauty impressed me? Not unless I had to pay for it, which I did quite often. It was not an unusual event when I paid for the company of women.

Sometimes I felt pain afterwards; a mental, sometimes emotional sort of pain. Not because I had cheated on my wife. I considered infidelity to be a natural act, something inevitable, timeless in its inevitability. It was timeless because it had been happening forever, to the best of men, both the ugly and the attractive, with reasons sometimes varying, other times quite similar. There was always a rationale.

For me…I was acting out of necessity, not spite's wickedness or lust's greed. I considered this the cruel nature of my place in the world. I was the embodiment of life's flawed composition. The hand of attraction I was dealt was a loser's hand, a hand so bad not even the greatest player could bluff his way to a victory. The garments of my appeal where made of a cheap, stylistically clashing sort of fabric and pattern, a flawed design that was never meant to make it through the test phase, onto the assembly line . The movie of my existence was a straight to video, dollar bin sort of quality. These were my sentiments on most days, sentiments that triggered the frustrations of self-pity, frustrations that drove me away from the warm walls of home cooking and towards the musky walls of a cheap motel, towards another disgruntled dive into the abused vagina of a broken soul.

Oh I know many will judge me to be a pathetic man, to be a man of no morals, no integrity, no loyalty or compassion for my wife. And I will not disagree. I am not a perfect man. I never have been. But what so many fail to comprehend is the frustration, the strain, the stress, the struggle that has long humiliated me. For years upon years, I possessed the same desires as the attractive people. I experienced the same tastes, the same visual wants, the same craving for intimate stimulation of the senses. I have forever held the beauty of a woman in the highest regard, upon a mantel above a fire that promised me the warmth of passion, an intensity of love which only the truly attractive can offer. Yet to be restricted from their affections, to be unable to satisfy such wants – what cruelty!

These various women I paid at various fees, these women provided a way for me to release the suppression of a dangerously growing need to feel something, some charge, some spark of life that my wife could no longer provide, or perhaps could never provide. I was able to momentarily realize fantasies that I had harbored since I was a young boy, ones that only grew in strength as my years increased.

This paying for the pleasure of women took a toll on me. That mental, sometimes emotional pain would knife its way through with the uncomfortable dullness of a butter knife. I would rather have had a legitimate affair. An affair would have built self-esteem rather than destroy it. An affair would have meant a beautiful woman shared similar emotions for me, a similar lust or desire for romance. An affair would have been sustainable, it would have provided me long term satisfaction in those areas I had felt so long deprived. Paying for sex leaves a man empty and alone. It is expensive masturbation.

When I was with these women, these various women I paid over the years, my fantasy was that they did somehow desire me naturally, without monetary influence. If the fantasy did not work, if I did not believe, if I was not convinced that that particular female was playing her part to my satisfaction, I would end the affair early, left to my despair, a couple hundred dollars poorer. Such was the rollercoaster ride of self-procurement.

While I am not a pretty man, I am also not a fit man. I suppose I am one of those men you barely notice. I am not hideous, but I am not handsome. I am just there. A filler in the population of life. Average.

I am also a shy sort of man. Not shy in the timid, innocent way, but shy in the way that I am unable to relate to those who are not me. Shy people are often quite charming once you get to know them. I am not sure I am one of those people. I have long understood that this has had much to do with my inability to have a legitimate affair. Women have never desired me, at least none whose beauty impressed me, nor have I had the confidence or the swagger to persuade them despite my various shortcomings.

I have never had many friends. None that I could say really knew me. None that really cared to know me. None that I cared to know. I have worked at the same company for over 15 years. Those are the people I know, who know me the best. Can't say I like many of them. And I am not a blind and stupid man, so I am quite certain the sentiments are mutual.

46

What is my job? What is it that I do? It's not important. Like my looks, it blends into the insignificant blah of life.

I'm not sure I would have even made acquaintances at work if it wasn't for my wife. When company events arrived on the calendar, I would insist we stay home, but my wife would insist we go, causing me to suffer a rising level of anxiety that triggered anger that led me to drink some whiskey but this did very little to slow the beat of my heart.

While attending these company events, my co-workers, these people I would rather avoid, they always engaged my wife. Or perhaps it was she who engaged them. Their reactions to her, especially upon a first meeting, were overly enthusiastic, as if utterly surprised my wife was such an amiable woman. The next day I would hear, "Wow, your wife is so nice" or "It was such a pleasure to meet your wife. She is so funny!" or "You are *such* a lucky man".

I suppose I comforted myself over the years with the thought that at least I was not alone. To be alone and unattractive and lacking confidence while consistently feeling alien to the *normalcy* of others, would be the sorriest state of all. What is one left with then? What does the unattractive man without friends or personality or any possibility of change, what does such a man have to live for?

***

The gun in my pocket, its steel barrel is cold. I run my finger down the ridge carved through the center, across its smooth side, over the safety, down the curve of the trigger.

I enter a forest preserve a few blocks from my house. Disappearing into the cover of its white foliage comforts me. I sit on a massive log, the remnants of a fallen tree, and scan the lifelessness of this forest. There are no tracks from squirrels on the hunt for food, no chirps from birds too confused to migrate before winter. I admire this lifeless beauty, its serenity, the peace of it all. I want to smile but I am unable.

I remove the gun from my pocket and lay it upon my lap. When I was a child I used to think guns were quite enchanting. They would inspire such fantasy. With a toy gun in my hand I transformed into something indestructible- fast, clever, ruthless in my ability to maintain what was just- eliminating the imaginary villains that threatened my home and my imaginary friends and that imaginary girl who with such beauty and vulnerability depended upon me for her protection.

Now... this gun... it is a terrible reality rather than an invincible fantasy. There will be no heroes in this tale. No innocent bystanders protected by its fierce honor. There is no beauty. There are no friends. And my home, no longer can I convince myself it is something worth protecting. This black and silver gun, a gun once used at some place in some time and in some way I will never know, it is soon to become participant to a tragedy.

What kind of tragedy?

It could be the tragedy of a man's inability to manage life; the tragedy of weakness, the fate of a man without free will-- that timeless tale of a man never having choice or a chance, a victim of circumstances, to forces beyond his control, a lonely man's soul long hijacked and driven by irrepressible demons.

Or perhaps it won't be a tragedy at all. Perhaps the mood will change and it will be the karma of one man's actions doing its due diligence. A life of amoral thought and action finally catching up with him in the form of divine justice. A cleansing of life's filth, so to speak.

Or perhaps, just perhaps, this will be a terrible drama that has not yet finished spreading its destructive wings upon those who happened to, and will happen to, cross a dying man's path.

I rub the cool barrel across the side of my face and am comforted by a final possibility. I gently push the tip of the barrel under the soft flesh that is beneath my chin, determining at exactly which angle I would have to tilt this gun to ensure the bullet rose with spinning destruction through the center of my brain.

I press the same tip of the barrel, now cooled by its kissing of my flesh, against the softness of my right temple. I imagine the explosion from the other side, the blood and brain fragments splattering the pristine whiteness of the forest. What a contrast: a colorful explosion of death spread like a masterpiece upon nature's white canvas.

And who would discover me? Someone always discovers a body. And what affect would my lifeless body, lying in the red snow, head blown in half, what affect would such a discovery have upon an individual? How would that horrific experience alter the course of their life? I imagine momentarily a beautiful woman, equally alone, perhaps also considering this often misunderstood need for permanent escape...perhaps this beautiful woman will love me in death...the sight of a broken man, alone in death, will inspire her to live. In death, a new life is born.

I consider this dark fantasy but it does nothing for me, offers no consolation.

***

It was 15 days ago. 15 days have followed. 15 days of absolute nothingness. For 15 days I have been the loneliest man in the world. Not a soul to call. Not a realistic hope to imagine.

I remember the morning quite vividly. I was in a terrible mood. I didn't want to go to work because I hated my job. I didn't want to wake because my bed was warm and my dreams were wealthy with limitless possibilities. My wife was her usual cheerful self. Energetic and optimistic, she was speaking enthusiastically about taking a trip in January, gifts she was thinking of buying me for Christmas, how peaceful I looked when I slept, how cute she thought I looked in the morning despite my "grumpy face". Oh, these lies I was so tired of hearing!

"Do I look fat in these pants?" My wife eventually asked.

I did not respond, my back turned towards her, my eyes closed.

"Hellloooo? I know you're awake, baby."

"Whu?" I mumbed.

"I asked you if I look fat in these pants."

I turned over, the bed squeaking, my frown concealed by the comforter.

"Yes," I said, looking her up and down, then turned back over.

She hadn't meant for me to be honest. She meant for me to tell her how beautiful she was, just as she always told me how sexy and adorable I was, despite the both of us knowing goddamn well we were lucky to be considered average.

My wife was gaining weight. More pounds to her already heavy frame. She'd been gaining weight for some time and it had been on my mind, so I figured *fuck it*, I'll tell her. Then maybe she'll stop going to Taco Bell and Burger King, maybe she'll start utilizing that health club membership I had bought her six months prior.

I heard pants being ripped off, hitting the floor, metal hangers sliding back and forth.

That morning my dick was hard when I woke. A young female had been in my dream, on my mind. Her name was Jenny and she was half my age. Her hair was blonde with shine, her eyes large with ambition, her breasts were small and firm with the ripeness of youth. I closed my eyes and could see the small curves of her ass, my fingers roaming free beneath the waistband of her panties.

"What about this outfit," my wife asked, a fresh attitude in her voice.

Squeezing my erect penis, I wished my wife would shut her mouth, disappear.

"Fucking hell, babe. You look great."

"How can you possibly say that without looking at me?"

My wife exited the room, slammed the bathroom door in the hall. My erection weakened

The day I met Jenny was the day I interviewed her. The department I managed needed another staff member. Details are not important. We were some smaller component of a larger component, all rather insignificant in the grand scheme of things. Such is the nature of the existence of most people, I now believe.

When she entered my office, I raised my swivel chair to it tallest height.   She sank into a low, worn chair before me.

It was those blue eyes, wide and pure, that blonde hair, styled straight like silk, those red fingernails, gripping a notebook tight with nervousness. It was the way she blushed pink and squeezed her thighs together. The way she smiled. She elevated me to a brand new place, brand new feelings.

I sat securely behind my beige metal desk, a desk not unlike the ones my teachers used in public school, a second hand desk with scrapes and dents and black marks scattered about. Jenny sat before me, her white teeth untainted by the signs of age- not yet yellow from coffee and cigarettes, not yet crooked from incessant grinding and dental neglect.

I withheld the comfort of a smile as I deadpanned at this young and attractive vision before me. I knew not how to react to her. There were too many thoughts, so much I was feeling. I was admiring so many things about this young girl. I remember her scent, some blended aroma of shampoo, lotion and perfume. How wonderful the scent of a female can be! The stiffness pressing tight against my Dockers was instantaneous and unrelenting as my sexual drive accelerated to a state I had not known and long forgotten since I was just a teenager.

Such striking features, such erotic perfume, such young uncertainty...

Behind me on the wall of my windowless office, hung two solitary items: a picture of my wife and I at a company picnic over seven years before, and a plaque congratulating me for being Salesman of the Year in 1993, over 12 years prior. As Jenny eyed the wall, I hoped her pretty blue eyes were focused on the latter.

"Wow, you won salesperson of the year in 1993?"

I nodded confirmation.

"Wow, that is like so impressive. How many other sales people were there?"

"Over 200," I said.

"200?!"

"Yes, over 200."

"That is incredible!"

I smiled a toothless smile.

"Promise me one thing, will ya? If I get this job, I mean if you decide to hire me, which of course we haven't even interviewed yet so like I know I am getting ahead of myself, for sure. But if I do get the job, you totally have to mentor me. I could be your apprentice. I really want to do well in sales. I mean, like I think selling stuff is sooo my calling. It's weird, like hard to explain. If you could teach me everything you know I would be soooo grateful."

The interview was a formality. For once, my 15 years of experience had finally influenced a decision worth something.
The energy I felt within my otherwise lethargic bones, the smile that lifted my otherwise heavy face and the possibilities that presented themselves within my otherwise limited capacity for imagination, made me feel as if a dark, cool cloud was sliding quickly from beneath a bright, hot sun.

A flood of scenarios, relentless with their vivid realness, inspired the stiffness in my pants and the quick lively beat in my heart. I wanted to run my fingers through her hair, my whiskers across her face, I wanted to slip my fingers in her blouse and across her breasts and I wanted her soft hands in my pants, her whispers in my ears, her warm body beneath mine. I wanted so much I could see it, feel it, hear the moans of our mutual journey towards the fulfillment of pleasure. I could see us in a hotel, on the bed, in each other's arms, watching late night television, not saying a word but just enjoying the comfort of each other's presence. I could see us in my car, my hands on her breasts as we drove quickly to our next sexual rendezvous, pressed for time, my wife calling because I am already late for dinner. Oh the thrill of it all; the thrill of all these fantastic possibilities.

I only knew her for an hour but I imagined Jenny loving a part of me I had never loved myself. She could love parts of me that proved that yes, I was a man worthy of beauty. She could love and adore me as my wife did, but it could be a love I embraced, just as I would embrace the pressing of her soft body on mine, her backside within the grasp of my hands, the warm moist surface of our tongues colliding.

This girl, this young and gorgeous Jenny, she became my young apprentice. Each morning and each late afternoon the wave of her perfume would rush into my office, sedating the pain of my self-pity and spark fire and substance into the cool chasm of my emotions.

In the beginning, it was as if I were in a dream. I couldn't have scripted the progress of our relationship better.

Initially we discussed the 'art of selling' and my advice greatly impressed her. Jenny was unaware that I was simply reading from an old book that had been buried deep within my desk drawer, regurgitating what it said, verbatim.

It wasn't long before I tired of discussing business and sought to move the conversations to topics more personal, more intimate.

"So tell me all about your weekend," I would say with a smile. And she would tell me in great detail what she had done, sometimes slightly outrageous, like the time she went skinny dipping with her friends while camping. Other times her stories were quite mundane, like how she hated the new season of Real World. But it didn't matter. All I wished for was for her to speak at length about something, which would allow me to be silent as I let my mind drift into another place, a place Jenny and I could share that was not the four walls of my office.

"So do you have a boyfriend?" I once asked.

"Well that's kind of personal, don't ya think?"

Quickly embarrassed, I felt my face turning red. I did not know what to say. I wanted to have a clever comeback, something that shrugged off her accurate observation with cool detached confidence.

Jenny straightened her long skirt so it covered the smooth skin above her thin knees. "It's cool," she smiled. "I'm bored with this work stuff too." I imagined my hand sliding across her knee, up her leg, under the smooth fabric of her skirt.

"Yes and no," she exhaled, eyes on the ceiling, palms pushing her thighs together, a strand of blonde hair kissing her left cheek.

53

"What does that mean?" I asked, a jealous insecurity rising vaguely within.

"I don't know. He's a jerk. Like technically he is my boyfriend, but... I don't know, he's just a total jerk sometimes."

I wanted to ask her if he beat her, if he cheated on her, if he was terrible in bed, if he bought her roses, took her to nice dinners, the movies, romantic weekends where he catered to her as if she were a princess. I wanted to ask because I wanted all the details. I wanted confirmation that I could furnish her better, I wanted to hate any man who had the opportunity to be intimate with Jenny because I was certain that my intimacy, our intimacy, would be like no other. I would treat her special, take her places, buy her things, rub and kiss those cute feet of hers, feet exposed by the open toed shoes she wore, caress that gentle skin of hers, the skin on her arms, the skin on her neck, on her back and face, gently across her thighs, that small stomach, tell her each day how special, how beautiful, how adorable and smart and funny she was. A relentless injection of affection and romance.

But I said nothing. I was unable to pursue such revelations about her boyfriend, unable to pull the words from mind to mouth, stuck in my own limited world of limitless possibilities.

"Sooo, what is your wife like?" Jenny once asked.

This question unnerved me. I preferred not to bring my wife into this world of ours. Considering my wife evoked such an array of conflicting emotions. Each time I had thought of my wife since the day I met Jenny, I would compare her to Jenny. My wife was fat, Jenny thin. My wife's nose was too big and somewhat crooked, Jenny's nose was small and straight, cute as a button. My wife's perfume suffocated stimulation, Jenny's electrified it.

"She's a real pain in my ass," I said, unsure how I would clarify such a strong statement.

"How so?" Jenny asked.

"She's a terrible cook," I said.

"She drinks too much," I frowned.

"She's lazy," I complained.

Jenny sat silent.

A desperate hope was the fire beneath each lie. I was slandering a woman who would have done anything for me. A woman I could never hate or even dislike for reasons of character.

"My wife doesn't want to better herself or to be anything special," I continued. "She has no aspirations for greatness."

Jenny remained silent.

I squeezed my sweaty hands together beneath the desk. Who *did* have aspirations for greatness?

My weak and desperate attempts to evoke sympathy were failing. Perhaps I had only portrayed myself as a failure of a man who had married a failure of a woman.

"She adores me though. She really does," I said with a smile.

"Really? What does she adore?" Jenny asked, sitting up in her chair, a smile now upon her face.

"Who knows," I smirked. "My cooking, the sweet things I do for her."

"What sweet things?" Jenny asked, an *awwww* tone in her voice. Her desire to know more inspired me to continue, to increase creativity.

"Poetry I suppose."

"You write poetry?"

"I guess."

"What do you mean, you guess? Either you do or you don't."

"I do. It's just weird talking about it. Kind of embarrassing, ya know?"

I had never written a poem in my life. My wife was the poet. I hated poetry.

"Oh that is like so silly!"

"What's silly?" I asked, feigning innocence.

"You! Not talking about your *passion*. I think it's so cool that you write poetry."

"You do?" A rush of blood through my penis moved it tight against my thigh.

"Yes! I think that is like so so cool. Can I read something you've written?"

"I don't know, I'm not sure it's very good."

"Oh I am sure it is. What do you know, anyway? Aren't artists like total perfectionists?"

I shrugged my shoulders.

"You *have* to bring me a poem."

"I *have* to, hugh?" The stiffness in my pants had reached a near unbearable fierceness. I needed to touch it, to squeeze and stroke it.

"Yes, like totally. All this time and my boss is a poet. Wow, that is like totally awesome."

I was in a sexually frenzied state. I craved Jenny stripped naked beneath me, the insanity of my erection penetrating her with rigorous repetition, her breasts bouncing, the squeeze of my hands upon them, my tongue stroking her nipples, my lips sucking them hard with passion, her moans crying wildly in my ears.

I knew I was in a dangerous world of fantasy. But this world in my head, this world inspired solely by the real existence of Jenny, this world that ignited a spark in my heart and fierce stimulation within my groin, this world was the happiest place I knew. And it was a world I wished to remain.

My wife stood across the room, pulling on her business casual slacks, concealing each repelling stretch mark, covering each pound of excess flesh.

"You can be a real jerk sometimes, you know that?"

I turned towards my wife. Her expression revealed hurt, anger.

"What are you talking about? You know I was only kidding."

"Whatever, Jim. You're a grumpy asshole sometimes. And I know you weren't kidding. You do think I'm fat."

"You're being crazy. We all gain a little weight when we get older. It's to be expected."

"So you think I only look a little fat?"

"I didn't say that. You look fine."

"Well if I look so fine, then why don't you desire me?"

"Hugh?"

"Why don't we ever fuck?"

"Jesus Christ, babe. What is up your ass this morning?"

"Right. Act stupid. Put this on me."

"Fucking relax, will ya?"

"You know you aren't much of a thoroughbred these days anyway. Even when we do fuck."

"And what the fuck is that supposed to mean?"

Silence.

"I *said*, 'what the fuck is that supposed to mean?'"

"I'm through with this conversation. It's stupid. I am going downstairs to make some breakfast. For myself."

I had the urge to call her a bitch, a fat bitch. But I resisted. Despite my anger, I knew my wife wasn't a bitch at all.

I did the only thing I could. I thought of Jenny. My beautiful, young Jenny. Jenny who's shirts were tight, her cleavage bare, her perfumes intoxicating.

There was a routine in my marriage. We never let the other leave the house without expressing our love. This was my wife's insistence because she always said, "One never knows what fate has in store for us."

When I descended the stairs that morning, my wife lingered by the front door, appearing to be on the verge of tears, awaiting my initiation of our routine. Without a glance in her direction, I continued on my way to the kitchen.

I heard a sniffle and the door slam. Good riddance, I thought. A tinge of guilt rose then fell weakly within.

On the way to work I thought entirely of Jenny, my young and beautiful apprentice. I was ready to take a chance on her. I was ready to ask her out to lunch, perhaps offer her a promotion, to escalate our intimate one on one's to the next level, to finally have the confidence to pursue the sexually romantic connection I had fantasized about countless times while seated on the toilet seat at home behind the locked bathroom door.

I was nervous when I arrived to work. I hadn't really considered the how's of what I was going to do. I figured I would simply ask her out to lunch. I would write her an email, something slightly professional but mostly personal. Why not, I thought. I knew I wouldn't have the confidence to succeed with her beautiful eyes watching my face as each premeditated word fumbled from my mouth.

58

I couldn't help but imagine the possibilities. We go to lunch, she admits having a crush on me, we rent a hotel, make love all afternoon...

I spent the entirety of the morning writing the perfect email. I would send it at 11:00; that way it would give her at least an hour to respond.

It was 10:30 when I received an email from my wife. She wrote that she loved me and apologized for over-reacting. She included a short poem at the end, something cliché and sentimental. She ended the email with the following: Our love is too strong to be diminished by such silly arguments.

Delete.

I returned to the email at hand. I closed my eyes and could see Jenny, smell Jenny, feel Jenny in my hands. I needed to write something clever, funny, smart. I had never written a flirtatious email before. What a dangerously exciting experience!

At 10:58 I was finished.

Send.

Five minutes went by...
Seven minutes...
Ten....
Twelve...
Fifteen...
Sixteen....

A new email arrived in my inbox. It was a notification that Jenny had opened my email. My heart began to race, legs started to shake. What if... What if... What if....

Jenny's desk was located around a bend, out of sight from my office. I knew I could walk over to her at any time, as I did quite often for various reasons, many contrived, but now I was terrified. I dreaded the seconds that ticked by as I waited for her to respond. What was she thinking? Feeling? How *would* she respond?

Eighteen minutes...
Twenty...

Twenty one...
Twenty two...

My phone rang and I answered. It was my wife.

"Hi sweety," she said.

"I'm busy," I responded coldly.

"But, I-"

"I'm on the other line, gotta go," I said.

"Oka-" I hung up before she could finish.

Why wasn't Jenny emailing me back? She had read the email over six minutes ago.

I comforted myself with the thought that maybe her response was lengthy. She wanted it to be perfect. I was overreacting. I just needed to give it time.

I decided to get out of my office for a few minutes, grab a glass of water, maybe a snack from the vending machine to calm my nerves. It was a long walk to the kitchen. People would say "Hi" and I would nod, forcing smiles that felt like grimaces.

I filled a cup of water, lifted its icy coldness to my lips with a trembling right hand and gagged as my throat rejected its cold passage.

I felt as if I were on the verge of something publicly catastrophic, something like a full-fledged anxiety attack, some public display that would expose the chaos of nerves that scurried wildly within. Eyes glued to the floor, I hurried into the seclusion of the bathroom.

The sight in the mirror did little to ease my condition. The thinning hairs on my scalp were falling, the bags beneath my eyes darkening, the dress shirt I was wearing was clinging cruelly to my 30 pounds of extra weight.

I splashed water in my face but felt no relief. My rising body heat was extracting what I feared would be the inevitable stench of perspiration. I tried to smile but I looked like some sort of maniac. My round cheeks looked strained. My thin lips were quivering. My teeth looked more crooked than usual, a darker yellow than what I remembered. I felt a tremble rising beneath the surface of skin on my face, a slight twitch flirting with spastic revolt.

What was becoming of me? Who was this man before me, this man on the verge of a breakdown? How was I going to take this girl out to lunch, to pursue this fantasy of mine? I couldn't even look myself in the mirror with any resemblance of sanity.

I needed a drink. Some sort of calming sedative. A reprieve from this anarchy of nerves. I prayed to a God I rarely acknowledged that she could not go to lunch, that she would email me back and tell me she had plans but she loved the idea and wanted to go another day, someday soon. At that moment I was entirely incapable of such a pressure filled interaction. I would need to drink at least a couple glasses of whiskey if I ever hoped to maintain a calming confidence. I knew this wasn't the ideal way to handle my anxieties but the alternative was much worse. This is an imperfect world with imperfect people who do imperfect things. A few cocktails would suppress destructive nerves and release the cool confidence necessary to build this crucial love affair.

I returned to my office. A hint of calm returned as I was now certain I would postpone this lunch affair for another time. I would respond to her acceptance with a sincere apology, perhaps an inside joke, something referring to the many conversations we had shared.

I opened my email. There was still no response from Jenny.

What the fuck! What was going on? Had I said too much? Was there something I said that was inappropriate?

I re-read my sent email dozens of times. Yes it was suggestive, but so what? It was nothing that could cost me my job. Sure I said she was a "cutey" and that I really enjoyed sharing "non-work related stuff" and that I could definitely "see us getting to know each other better outside the stuffiness of this office". What was wrong with that?

I closed my door and paced my small office. Sweat ran as my body heat rose. I felt like punching the wall, kicking my desk, smashing my computer. I bent down and shut off my monitor. I couldn't stand to watch my inbox.

Less than a minute went by and I couldn't bare it any longer, so I sat down, turned my monitor back on. I noticed an email from my wife. The subject line read: *I love you so much, sweety.*

I refused to read it. I didn't care. I knew she loved me. So what? I heard it every fucking day. Enough already for Christ's sake! She was nothing but an average man's settlement, an acceptance of mediocrity, a fat wife with average looks. Who dreams of that? Who considers such a vision to be their ideal *soul mate* when growing from teens to twenties, when jerking off to porn, when rubbing the stiffness of a young cock, eyes closed, reality dictated by the limitless possibilities of fantasy? Show me one and I'll call them a liar!

Was my wife blind to this? No one is *that* blind, I am certain. And why did this woman love me so? Was I not the same for her? Was she not lying to me each morning she said I was adorable and each evening she wormed her way across the bed and slid her warm arms around me? Was not my reliance upon those arms wrapped around me, that warmth of her body against mine, that sense of calm I succumbed to – was that not undeniable proof that I was nothing more than a desperate man? With a desperate woman? Two people scorned by the cruel stroke of life's cruel design?

Oh sure, I could take the path of depth, of religion or spirituality- whatever you may call it – and I could say some ridiculous cliché about how beauty is from within. But I won't! I was an unhappy man!

It was now 11:55

Should I walk over to her desk? What would I say? What a tease she has been!

11:56

Did I love this girl? Or did I just want to fuck her? Or was it both? Oh what a desperate man I was!

11:57

I needed to get out of there. This girl was too far beneath my skin, too deep within my head.

11:58

My eyes were closed and I could see it all: In a hotel. Or the backseat of my car in a forest preserve. Or making love in her apartment. Or in my bed when my wife wasn't home. I could divorce my wife and we could marry – I could live the life I never had a chance to live before... youthful and wild and filled with sex and laughter, free from the doldrums of a *have not* existence. If this bitch would only email me back!

11:59

I stood up, swung open my door and walked to her cube. She was not there. I asked the others where she had gone. They gave me strange looks, told me she had gone out to lunch. With *who*? I asked, more agitated and louder than I had anticipated. They said they didn't know. Her boyfriend, they thought. Her *boyfriend*, I said. They were staring. I was hot, felt red, sweat quickly returned to my forehead and beneath my arms.

12:03

In my car, I was on the way to the bar. I needed something to relieve this madness that had taken control of me. What a *bitch* Jenny was. What a goddamn, insensitive *bitch*. It was common courtesy to respond to someone who invited you to lunch. I could have given her a promotion, made her a team leader, made recommendations for future jobs. I could have written a poem for her because I no longer hated poems because I had finally felt love and that was what poetry was about, right? Writing about love? Did this bitch realize any of these things? Of course not!

4:45

My cell phone rang as the bartender slid me another shot, another beer.

"What do you want for dinner," my wife asked.

I told her I didn't know. She asked where I was. I told her I was unwinding at the bar, it had been a rough day.

"What happened?" she asked.

"I don't want to talk about it," I said.

"Are you sure?" she asked

"Yes, goddamnit, Are you deaf?" I shouted.

She hung up, tears likely rolling over and down her fat cheeks. I could care less. I chased a shot of whiskey with half a pint of beer.

I scanned the newspaper in front of me, searched the local adult ads. I needed a girl. Fuck the two hundred dollars. My sexual drive craved the release into any woman who was not my wife.

I called several ads before I found one who agreed to meet me at the Days Inn at 8:00.

My wife called back, noticeably upset, and told me she was leaving, that she'd be home in 30 minutes. She offered to pick up my favorite dinner on the way home – KFC. I said sure, why not.

When I arrived home I retrieved a porno magazine from my closet and masturbated. For several weeks I had been thinking about Jenny but now I was livid at the thought, so I concentrated on fucking the women who were grimacing from the slick pages beneath me. But now the fantasy, all fantasy, was less real, more impossible. I failed to finish.

My wife was late. I figured she was trying to prove some point, deciding to work late to spite me. So I drank a beer. Then another. And then another. Two hours passed and I called her at work. No answer.

I had to leave soon to meet the girl from the ad. I couldn't wait for my wife and her goddamn KFC.

I needed some real sex, some real touch, a real body moaning beneath mine.

I called my wife's cell phone.   No answer.

I called again- no answer.

Called again –finally a man answered.

"Who the fuck is this," I said, livid, drunk.

"This is Officer Thompson.   Who am I speaking with?"

"This is Jim Feely.   I am trying to get in touch with my wife."

"Jim, we've been trying to track you down."

"What are you talking about?"

"You better meet us at the hospital."

"What?   Why?   What has happened?"

"You better meet us at the hospital."

"Goddamn you!   What the fuck has happened!"

"There had been an accident, Jim.   Your wife is dead."

Bullets in the gun.   The gun in my hand.   What a frigid morning it has become, the sun now concealed by the thickness of clouds.

I stand from the log and walk along the inner edge of the forest.   My eyes are shut as I search for one good reason to exist.

Suddenly I experience the semblance of a smile.   A faint rush of warmth.   I think I feel something.   Memories begin to return.   I can see her smile.   Her laughter.   Her understanding.   Her honesty.   I can see us together and I can see the moments we have yet to have.   I am comforted by possibility.   By the chance of misunderstanding.   By the vision of her pity that leads to her love that brings us together.

I rush back to my house and start my car.   I speed for what seems like days, eventually arriving.

I rush inside. People are shocked to see me. I hear, "I'm so sorry"; I hear, "If there's anything I can do"; I hear, "So good to see you back". I am not as sad as the expressions that rotate before me. Quite the contrary. I am alive with joy, rejuvenated and reborn with hope, I can see a destiny that will return me from the edge of ruin and raise me to brand new heights of happiness.

I run to her desk and drop to my knees. I tell her that she means the world to me, that I love her. She is in tears as I pick her up, swing her around, press my trembling lips against hers. We run out laughing, crying, blind to the scene that surrounds us. In my car we are kissing, hugging, touching, promising.

We drive like a blur to my house.

We make love on the couch, then on the bed, her perfume is now my perfume, her sweat my sweat. We shower together and I lather the smooth skin on her young body. She tickles me, I tickle her, we laugh. After I dry her off we re-enter the bed, hold one another, love one another. It's all so silly and cliché, so perfect.

I open my eyes and the snow has been falling heavy and thick. My tracks are now gone. The barrel of the gun is bruising the roof of my mouth. I close my eyes and I am again making love to this young girl, this young apprentice of mine, this love I so cherished, this fantasy I so longed to feel as something real. It is hard to smile with a gun in my mouth, but I manage.

My index finger is firm upon the smooth curve of steel. A winter gush lashes my cooling skin. The images of Jenny are quickly fading. I see nothing but a cold bed in an empty home. And I pull the trigger.

The Seed

A couple not pretty. Maybe not cool. But in love. She adores him and he adores her when he's not infatuated by the women with the bodies and the smiles and the styles. A self-conscious couple. I can see that as I dip my mind into their world as I sit alone in mine. What is real and what is simply an imagining of the chaotic wiring of mind and memory?

A meth addict serial killer on the run. 8 people dead. A family of four. A 65 year old man with a car behind a grocery store. A friend and that friend's friend. A lover. Maybe more. He's got tattoos and blood on his shirt and a shaved head and wild eyes. Victims all died of blunt trauma to the head. He carries a 9mm. He's in the vicinity. That's what the media says.

Nondescript jazz playing boringly through the café speakers. Nothing that cuts to the core of original. Nothing Miles Davis on heroin. A woman behind me talks of divorce over the phone while taking sketchy notes on a makeshift piece of paper. Something about there being no difference between having her ring on or not having it on…either way she looks down and is reminded of things she'd rather forget. She annoys me and I wonder what the point of her existence is.

A pretty black girl walks through the door and I believe with a burst of something that I could love her. That under different circumstances she could love me. A different time. A different place.

My neck sweats and the hood of this sweatshirt clings to my face. It's too small. Not my size. But who has time to choose when they steal? It does the trick I suppose. I need a shave. That would help. Some sunglasses. The not cool lovers in front of me are looking. When my eyes meet theirs they look away. Are they reading the same internet news story I am?

An elderly couple sits with coffee and mutual kindness and a Danish to share. He is selfless and gentlemanly and she is gentle and appreciative. May God spare their souls for returning to a state of purity at this moment in time. Does it really take 80 years to return? Are we ever there or is it something about death's doorstep that finally delivers truth and love?

Pants not mine. Shirt not mine. Sweatshirt not mine. Shoes not mine. Money not mine. Truck not mine.
Hands shake. Teeth motion at a slow grind. Eyes full and wide and black. What a life.

When it ends and we know it's going to end but we have some time to act prior, do we calculate something grand or do we let it come as it may without concern for some final statement? When life has dealt you a rather wicked hand and you can recall with uncertainty those episodes of effort where you tried so goddamn hard to turn it around and pick up the rectangular bricks of good instead of the jagged stones of bad, what do you do in your final stretch before extinction?

I'm so damn tired. I close my eyes. Rest my heavy head against the wall. Fold my arms and squeeze my triceps. There once was a place. A tree, some flowers, a little sunshine, a few kind voices… and just a little bit of love. I know this. I can recall it with wishing but nothing else. But it's real. Once before, but so distant and so temporary. Like the seeds of a flower that should have died from some planted pesticide but morph into something rather grotesque and unwanted, like a weed that harms the beauty of a garden and must be destroyed at its very root before it destroys the rest, the gorgeous, the good, the wanted.

I open my eyes and I am alone. The not cool couple is gone. The elderly lovers have left their seats empty but their Danish and coffees full.   The black girl has disappeared as if she were only an apparition and never real. Bright lights blaze through the window. So many colors. And then so many faces. So many demands. So much intensity. All I want to do is sleep. To pretend my seeds are blossoming and my leaves will one day be pretty and green.

King

I found myself in a room with several naked young women. All of them were on drugs, my drugs, the drugs I purchased for this wild party. Many of these females were paid for and I loved them for that. I loved the way they touched one another and the way they danced with each other and I adored the innocent evil in their eyes as they watched me get head from three of their peers.

The psychotic strobe on the ceiling flickered mad movements slow motion.

Through a gigantic ceiling mirror I watched myself elevated on a golden platform, sunken into my large red velvet chair, soaring through my galaxy of ecstasy, cocaine and Viagra.

Three young prostitutes with hair red white and blue were trying desperately to ejaculate my superhuman cock.

I felt like a King, in my Kingdom, with my girls, my drugs, my pinnacle of pleasure.

Then I woke to the narrowness of a single bed under the flicker of a dying bulb in a Bangkok motel.

Lost

I awoke dehydrated with a headache and the taste of a late night gyro on my breath. I was not in my bed, not in my apartment. There was a strange girl in my arms- a petite girl- a girl with the skin and face and hair of India.

The beige sheets had been shoved to the edge of the bed and my unclothed body was exposed.

The clock on the wall read 6am.

The room was warm and stuffy and small. There was a miniature TV propped up on a TV dinner stand at the foot of the bed and to my left there was a black fridge and a black stove with a small white sink stuck between. The walls were a faded grotesque brown.

Beige Venetian blinds heavy with dark dust were only half drawn, the rising sun slightly visible as it began to burn in the early morning sky.

There were mirrors. Mirrors everywhere. Mirrored closet doors, a mirrored ceiling above the bed, a mirrored coffee table, mirrors hanging on the walls, even a hand held mirror lying on the floor next to my white boxers. Nearly every mirror reflected the scene of me, as if I were a spectator viewing my own life, my own situation exactly as it was. A perspective some should never have. It's a discomforting perspective. It reveals too much, it's too raw, too cruel in its blunt delivery.

I glanced at each mirror and in each one I was forced to watch my soft sedated penis lying lifeless on my inner right thigh. I slid it between my legs and turned over, away from the majority of mirrors.

I was now facing a strange girl. Her round dark eyes gazed at my discomfort with an unsettling liveliness. I felt hot and nauseous and confused.

"Morning," she said as if she'd been up for hours.

I moaned, rubbed my head, wished I was not so exposed.

She smiled with energy, her eyes big, her demeanor comfortable, at ease.

I tried to snag and pull the beige sheets with my foot but failed, knocking them to the floor instead.

She snuggled closer to me. Hotter against me. I kissed her on the forehead but had no idea why. With my kiss her smile fell softly and her eyes closed gently. She looked happy. She looked content.

Her right breast was hanging, her nipple hard. I ran my finger across the nipple, pinched it with my fingers. Her smile returned and her eyes remained shut. When I touched her I felt the absence of stimulation. Just skin against hand. Cold against hot.

I kissed her softly on her cheek and her smile grew and she wrapped her small legs around my right knee and slowly gyrated up and down, her not soft pubic hair brushing me like bristle. She kissed me on the cheek. Her lips were hot and dry. I watched the live feed of us in the mirror above the bed. I was pale looking. I needed to trim my pubic hair. I was tired looking. She had dark hair. Everywhere. In places I didn't wish to see dark hair. Her forearms, her face, even her neck. Not a lot of hair, but enough to notice.

She looked up into the mirror and watched me watching her. She stroked the hair on my chest, watched the strokes as they happened live in the mirror, pleased by the action on display. I watched her watching me, thought she was probably quite cute under different circumstances. She resumed her gyrations and I felt wetness spread against my leg. I rubbed her inner thigh, skimmed her moist vagina. She moaned something I could not decipher and gazed at me with intensity- a look I could not determine to be the look of a girl in love or a girl who just liked to fuck.

My mouth was dry. I craved some food to soak the alcohol that filled my stomach.

She grabbed my dick, which was cool and soft and small. Her hand was hot, semi-moist and sticky. She squeezed and stroked my dick, but it was unresponsive, not interested, it had to go to the bathroom.

I sucked on a tit, trying to divert her from touching my dick, wondering what the hell I was doing sucking on her tit when it did nothing for me. She grabbed my dick again and yanked with more force, with an increased determination to spark an erection. I squirmed from her yanking gasp and stuck a finger in her, kind of hard, kind of forceful. She moaned loud, begged for more fingers. This moan sort of turned me on and I felt my dick begin to rise with warmth. I fingered her with two more fingers, bit her left tit, and she moaned louder, gyrated her pussy into the jab of my fingers slow and fast and hard and soft.

I thought about fucking her. I thought about the condom I didn't have. I tried to remember whether or not I had fucked her the night before.

She squeezed my ass and I kissed her neck and she moaned and I closed my eyes and she begged for me to be inside her and I felt like I was going to throw up from all the movement, all the alcohol swishing and swashing back and forth in my stomach, but my dick was stiff and suddenly wanting, so I climbed on top of her. She spread her short legs wide and my dick pointed to her pussy. She smirked and bit her bottom lip. I slid my hung-over hard-on into the darkness of her pussy, a pussy whose lack of grooming I suddenly didn't mind, kind of liked in a strange new way. Her eyes rolled back and I squeezed her little ass and she growled. I quickly got a rhythm going. She cussed dirtier words than fuck, she scratched, she made a chameleon-like range of faces that conveyed begging, thanking, warning, hating, loving, needing, fearing, demanding. I was enjoying the sex but couldn't help wonder what sort of STD I was catching. I fucked hard and fast, tried to cum as quickly as possible. She sensed this, telling me to cum inside her. I said no. She said yes. I came inside her.

We laid there in silence. Five minutes passed and then she giggled. I asked her what was so funny. She said nothing. I asked her if she did this a lot. She asked me what I meant. Fuck strange guys. She assured me with a smile that she had never done this before, that she had never brought home a strange guy. I didn't believe her but I wanted to. I asked her if she took birth control. She said sometimes. I asked what that meant. She said they should be fine. I wanted to leave.

I asked if she had any aspirin and she said yes, in the bathroom, so I climbed out of the bed and walked dizzy and annoyed, my bare feet stepping across a layered floor of dirty clothes.

Her bathroom was filthy. Dark rings around the toilet. A thick grime accumulated on the sink. Clothes and hairs scattered everywhere. I opened her cabinet and noticed a large bottle of KY Jelly next to her Advil. It was empty. *Jesus Christ*, I cursed. I swallowed six Advil and stared into the filthy mirror. The reflection irritated me.

I pulled back the shower curtain. A musty smell permeated the air and I gagged. Quickly, I grabbed a bar of soap and turned on the faucet. I splashed my dick with cold water and scrubbed rigorously. After rinsing, I scanned the bathroom for a towel. I found only one, a tan one on the floor with brown stains on it. I used sheets of toilet paper instead.

I desperately wanted to leave but I had no idea where I was. My watch read 5:15 and I doubted I could easily find a cab, so I reluctantly returned to the bed, nausea making me sweat and light headed and depressed.

I laid down, my eyes watching the live feed of me on the ceiling. I closed my eyes but the spinning and nausea intensified. I opened my eyes and she was watching the live feed of me. I was watching the live feed of her, of us. I watched her squirm her way beneath my reluctant arm and I watched me hold this young Indian girl snuggled tight against me. The six Advil slowly took effect and I eventually fell back asleep.

I awoke again in two hours and she was in the shower. I clothed myself clumsily, made sure I wasn't forgetting any essentials like my wallet or my phone or my watch, and I exited her apartment into a dark and smelly hallway. I made my way to the street and scanned the neighborhood, recognized nothing.

I walked several blocks, turning left, turning right, heading straight… searching for the promise of a major intersection. After walking fast and angry and sick and tired for nearly thirty minutes, I yelled "fuck!" into the quiet the morning.

I considered returning to the Indian girl's apartment but didn't have a clue where that was, nor did I care to know. A few minutes later I happened upon a major intersection and found my cab.

Once home, I paid the cabbie and walked slowly up the steps to the door. I repeatedly rubbed my dick through my pants, wondering if I was feeling any sensation like an itch or a burn.

I entered the apartment quietly and heard sobbing. I walked slowly towards the bedroom and noticed how clean and neat the apartment was. How nice it smelled. I walked by the bathroom and glanced in. I was comforted by the clean hanging towels and the spotless sink.

Reaching the bedroom, I stood in the doorway. The tired red face of my fiancé looked up from a wet pillow and the expression moved quickly from fear and sorrow to rage. I scanned the room and noticed there were no mirrors. And the Caribbean blue we chose for the walls was beautiful.

Where the fuck have you been, she asked.

Lost, I mumbled.

Streets

He drove and drove and drove. Past his old house. Through the streets of dreams and memories that were his home until he was 12. He drove slowly. He felt the hint of peace as a smile struggled through his tense face.

Those streets were called Mother.

He left that humble neighborhood and drove into the hills, where the houses were larger and the memories darker. He felt pain and insecurity. Anger ripped through him. The engine beneath the hood of his Mercedes roared as he sped away.

Those streets were called Father.

Three Sounds

The sun burns bright in the ocean blue sky. The suburb is blossoming green with trees immersed in the promise of their transformation, the birth of yet another cycle of life. A couple in their early 40's kneels in front of their home, nurturing the seeds of a summer garden with water and hope, sweat and uncertainty. A young couple wheels their newborn down the sidewalk, their coffees full, their baby asleep. They glance down at their creation and smile in unison. He kisses her and she closes her eyes, moves closer to him.

Kelly looks out her second story window and watches her mother and father kneeling in the garden. She's on the phone with her friend Kristen.

"I don't know," Kelly says, "it's like I want to go to this party and yeah I can totally drive, but-"

"But what?" Kristen interrupts. "This is like supposed to be the best freakin party all year. Not some lame ass sophomore party where you drink beer in a park or sit around and watch boys play Wii in their basement. This is the real deal Kristen."

"I know, trust me I'm totally with you on this. It's just that I have an early curfew and –" Kelly looks down once more at her parents and shakes her head, "well, my parents wanted me to go to the Apple Orchard with them and my granny and my little brother."

Kristen erupts in laughter. "Could you be any more *gay*? Jesus Christ – are you like 9 years old or something?"

Kelly is watching her father teasing her Mom, chasing her, wiping dirt on her face. They are both laughing.

"Yeah I guess you're right," Kelly says.

"Of course I'm fucking right," Kristen laughs. "We'll get you home by your curfew, don't worry. It's only a pool party and it starts on 3. That gives us plenty of time to find a man to fondle us."

Kelly laughs sort of forced, sort of nervous.

"Will I know anyone there?" Kelly asks.

"Sure, you'll at least recognize people. I mean we do all go to the same school, you know. Besides, I will totally introduce you to some people. I'm sure a senior stud would love a little piece of your young booty."

"You think so, hugh?" Kelly says a little sarcastic, a tinge hopeful, mostly fearful.

"Most def, girlfriend. You got a nice little booty on you and that cute innocent thing going on."

Kelly says nothing, scratches the back of her head, looks down at her parents in the garden, focused and dirty.

"Anyway," Kristen says. "You are going to this party because if you don't go, then I don't have a ride and therefore cannot go. Comprende?"

Kelly hangs up with Kristen and walks to a partially removed poster of Hannah Montana. She glances at it for a moment and sort of smiles, then takes it down and places it in a large black trash bag. She does the same with her Jonas Brothers posters, as well as an old Dora the Explorer poster she had been holding on to for years. She then places each of her stuffed animals in the same trash bag and throws the bag into the hallway, ready to be taken to the attic.

The phone rings and it's Stephanie. Stephanie has been in gymnastics with Kelly for the last 6 years and is her closest friend.

"Hey girl," Kelly says.

"Hey Kell-Kell! What are you doing?"

"Cleaning," Kelly says.

"Awesome," Stephanie says. "I just did that this morning. Hey – whatcha got going on tonight? Wanna rent a movie or something?"

Kelly rubs her face, scratches her ear and says "I can't. Wish I could. I'm not feeling that good."

"Oh, sorry to hear that," Stephanie says.

"Yeah, like I need to run right now because I think I'm gonna puke."

Kelly sits in front of her computer and logs into Twitter as "gymnastics diva".

Kelly tweets: *feel bad, totally lied to friend.*

76

Kelly tweets: *Kristen is cool. Sometimes wonder if she likes my car more than me :(*

Kelly tweets: *should I go to senior pool party????*

Kelly tweets: *won't know ANYONE! But maybe meet a cute boy :-)*

Kelly first met her friend Kristen at the Dairy Queen on Lake Street after school four weeks ago. Kelly was at the DQ with her little brother, William, when Kristen tapped her on the back of the arm.

"Hey sexy sophomore chic," Kristen said loudly through the chaos of boys and girls who were pushing and flirting and smoking and laughing.

"We've got 4th period English together don't we?" Kristen asked.

"Oh yeah, totally," Kelly said. "Yup, I thought you looked familiar."

"Cool cool – this must be your lil bro, hugh? Goddamn he's cute!" Kristen flicked her cigarette to the ground and winked at William.

"You drive, hugh?" Kristen asked, looking back towards the parking lot. "That's wicked you got a car. I wish I had a car. Sure makes things easier not having to hoof it everywhere. "

Kelly smiled, felt sort of guilty, told Kristen that if she ever needed a ride to just let her know.

"Give me your digits," Kristen said immediately.

Kelly looks in her bedroom mirror, examines her small breasts, runs her hands over her small backside. She winks at the mirror and then feels silly and sits back down to her computer.

Kelly tweets: *Kristen is cool. Kinda wild but I like cause my life is totally borrring.*

Kelly tweets: *room almost totally clean. Can't believe I still have a mini mouse clock! Totally embarrassing! Whatif Kristen saw it!*

Kelly tweets: *gonna tell parents im goin to mall untl seven, then kristen's til nine.*

Kelly tweets: *totally goin to party! Apple orchards are lame. Senior pool party would be sooo fun*

Kelly tweets: *wonder if alcohol will be there. Totally not drinkn. Tried dad's beer once and OMG it was GROSS!*

Kelly then text messages Kristen: *Be ready soon!*

A car's engine starts and the loud melody of a chart topping pop song pierces the quiet calm of the late Saturday morning. The small engine of a Kelly's two-door Toyota whines as it reverses out of the long driveway. Kelly nearly hits the fence on the left, then the window well on the right, then rolls partially over the front lawn. Eventually Kelly stops at the request of her father. He has dirty hands and sweat on his brow. The passenger window rolls down and the pop song screams into the air. The young couple on their way back home looks over sort of annoyed, sort of amused. The baby is still asleep.

"Turn the music down, Kelly," her father says loudly.

Kelly rolls her eyes and turns the music down.

"Looks like your backing up skills need a little work. Or maybe we should buy the house next door, tear it down and expand our driveway," he teases.

"Whatever Dad, I'm getting better. At least I didn't hit the fence."

"This is true," he says. "So where are you headed off to?"

"Shopping," Kelly says, her fingers on the volume dial.

"Shopping where?"

"The *mall* Dad. Where else would I shop?"

"Don't get smart with me, young lady. It's a simple question."

"I'm *not*," Kelly whines defensive.

Kelly's father wipes the sweat from his face, leaves a streak of dirt behind.

"Who are you going with?" he asks.

"Kristen."

"Who?"

"My new friend Kristen. Don't worry, I won't be with boys.

"You sure?" he says, sort of teasing, sort of serious.

"I'm not a slut Dad."

Kelly's father looks perplexed, leans into the car.

"Don't be so melodramatic, Kelly. You know I don't think such crazy things. You are 16 and I have the right to know where you are going and who you are going to be with."

"You always say I am being dramatic. I mean whatever Dad. I'm going with Kristen and we are going to the mall and I'll be home by nine. *Okaaay?"*

Kelly's cell phone beeps, she looks at it and sighs *"as if"*.

"Who is that?" her father asks.

"Nobody," Kelly says, annoyed, and puts the car in reverse. "Can I *go?*" she says without patience.

Her father opens the door abruptly, leans in, slides the shifter into park, kills the engine and rips the keys from the ignition.

"Get out of the goddamn car," he orders through his teeth, his eyes fierce.

Kelly is defiant and crying in the kitchen. Her father is red faced and pointing to the stairs.

"You aren't going anywhere until you can learn to respect your parents!" her father screams.

Kelly's mother stands by her husband with a loyal scowl, gloves from the garden tight in her hands.

Kelly runs up the stairs screaming, "I hate you! I hate you!" – the final *hate you* more like a shriek. Her father moves to follow Kelly up the stairs, astonishment and anger in his face. Her mother grabs his arm and quietly orders him to let her go, to let her emotions calm, to let his emotions calm.

Her father walks with his wife to the family room and sits down. He looks at her for an answer. She rubs his shoulder and sort of smirks.

"This isn't funny," he says.

"I know," she smiles.

"It's not. I mean what the hell happened to our sweet little girl? We didn't raise this monster?"

"I know honey. It's just a phase. 16 is a confusing time for young girls. I'm sure she'll grow out of it by the time she is 25." The wife kisses her husband on the cheek. "Just 9 more years of this, no sweat," she smiles.

"Very funny. You always know just the right thing to say."

Kelly's little brother, William, is in her room reading one of her books when she enters.

"Get out of my room," she cries.

"Why?" William asks with faint defiance.

"Because I said so! Did you ask me to be in my room?"

"No," he says submissively.

"Then get out!" Kelly screams.

William throws the book to the floor. "You're a witch," he says under his breath as he walks to the door. Kelly whacks him across the head and pushes him out the door. William starts crying and Kelly slams the door.

Kelly lies on her bed and pulls her iPhone from her purse. She opens the Twitter app and tweets: *I so wish I was 18 now so I could move outt!!!*

Kelly switches her CD to Avril Lavigne and lies back down on the bed.

She tweets: *I hate my parents SOOOOO much*

She tweets: *my parents hate me. I hate them. Totally done with it ALL!!*

She tweets: *anyone out there in twitter world who hates their parents as much as ME?!?!?!!?!?!?*

Kelly's phone rings and it's Kristen.

Kristen: What's up bitch? Where are you?

Kelly: My Dad is being a total dick. He says I have a bad attitude and I need to learn to respect him. Give me a break. Does he respect *me*? I think not!"

Kristen: Well, you do have a shitty attitude.

Kelly: No I don't!

Kristen: Don't wig out bitch -I was only kidding. They are probably miserable because they hate each other. Too bad they don't realize they are fucking up their kids with their goddamn misery.

Kelly: They actually get along really well.

Kristen: Yeah right. All married people are miserable, some just lie better than others. Ask mine. Best thing they ever did was get divorced. Only took them 20 years to do it!

Kelly: My parents aren't going to get divorced. Trust me. It's gross how much they love each other.

Kristen: Whatever. Just stab them, make it look like an accident and collect your inheritance.

Kelly: What?

Kristen: Totally kidding. Don't get all sensitive on me. Just a joke.

Kelly: Whatever. Looks like I'm grounded for the night.

Kristen: Are you kidding me? What about Trevor's party?

Kelly: What do you want me to do? Murder my parents so I can get out of this house and go to the party?

Kristen: Yes! Poison them!

Kelly: Jesus Christ.

Kristen: No use in calling Jesus 's name. He's not going to get you to Trevor's party. Unless whores are there. I heard Jesus loved whores.

Kelly: Are you insane!? Jesus did not love whores.

Kristen: *Eeezy* catholic bitch, I was like totally joking. Don't work your anus into a spicy wing shitting frenzy!

Kelly: You are like so *crude.*

Kristen: Listen, you better go kiss your Dad's ass and tell him you're sorry for being a bitch. You can *not* miss this party.

Kelly: I am not kissing his ass. I did nothing wrong.

Kristen: How the hell am I supposed to get there without you? You are my ride. Besides, Mike fucking Donovan is going to be there. I totally plan on giving him some sucky tonight.

Kelly: Sucky?

Kristen: Yeah bitch, sucky on his beautiful tan athletic steroids cock!

Kelly: You are nasty. You really plan on giving him a blowjob? He's 18 and not to mention I heard he's had more women than Tiger Woods.

Kristen: Whatev! That means he's got experience. And he knows how to use a long stick.

Kelly: Jeez Louise – you sound like a total slut.

Kristen: Oh whatever Kelly, you know I am totally joking. I'm not that big a slut. Well, maybe a little bit but at least I've got good taste. It's not like I'd sucky just anyone.

 Kelly: Okaaaay

Kristen: Whatev prude bitch. You've probably never seen a dick before.

Kelly: I am not a prude. I just haven't found a guy I'm ready to get intimate with.

81

Kristen: Intimate? Who the uses words like that? Are you a lesbo?

Kelly: Nooo! I just want it to be special.

Kristen: Awwww, that's so cute. Well you can be perfect while I have fun tonight. Just get over here and pick me up.

Kelly: I will see what I can do with my Dad.

Kristen: Make it happen. I am totally not missing this party tonight!

Kelly: I'll call you back.

Kelly's mother knocks on the door and asks to come in.

"It's not locked Mom."

Her mother sits on the bed next to her daughter.

"Everything okay, sweetie?" her mother asks.

Kelly stretches back on the bed and sighs, "yes Mom, I'm just fine. No need to get all dramatic."

"You've been awfully moody lately. Kinda distant. Is everything okay at school?

Kelly nods her head with a sarcastic affirmative, her face in her iPhone. She tweets: *my mom is like so clueless!*

Her Mom puts her hand on Kelly's knee and softly asks, "is there anything going on that maybe I can help you with? You know I was 16 once too."

"Really? You were? I thought you were like *always* old," Kelly says sarcastically.

"Real funny young lady," her mother says with a smile.

"Mom," Kelly softens slightly. "I wish I could tell you something to make you feel better, but I don't know what you want me to say. Nothing is wrong with me."

"That's okay. You don't have to figure it out right now."

"Figure *what* out?" Kelly says, face still in her iPhone. She tweets: *mom so annnnoyying!!!*

"Relax honey. We just worry about you, that's all. That's what parents do. Some day when you have your own little Kelly growing up so fast and all of a sudden driving and going out to strange places, then you'll know why we get a little – how do the kids say it these days – tripping?"

Kelly laughs, says "Yeah, that pretty much sums it up I guess. Tripping."

"See – I'm pretty hip. I haven't always been an old dork."

"Not always old anyway," Kelly laughs as her Mom pulls her close and hugs her, kisses her on her head.

"We love you very very much, sweetie. We just want to make sure you are always safe and happy."

"I *know* Mom," Kelly says, sort of defensive, sort of uncomfortable.

"So what's your new friend Kristen like?" her mother asks.

"She's cool," Kelly says. "Like a straight A student and somewhat of a prude with guys. Some think she is a lesbian because she doesn't put out."

"Well that's just stupid. Hopefully they think the same about you," her mother says hopeful.

"That I'm a *lesbian*?"

"No no no, that you don't put out."

"Oh," Kelly says.

"You don't, do you?" Kelly's Mom asks, pretending she is joking by asking.

"Nooooo Mom. Wow, your trust is like so strong."

"No need to get defensive honey. I was just teasing you. I know you are a good girl."

"Good," Kelly says sarcastically.

Kelly's Mom looks around, notices the posters no longer on the walls, says nothing. She then puts her hand on Kelly's knee and says, "I spoke with your Dad and we are okay with you going out this afternoon as long as you apologize to him."

"Really?"

"Yes, really."

"Okay," Kelly says with a rising mood.

Moments after her Mom leaves, Kelly's little brother, William, knocks on her door. She tells him to come in.

"Hey," he says. "I made this for you."

William hands Kelly a pink bracelet he has made by dying white shoelaces and twisting them together.

"Wow," Kelly says with a smile. "This is sooo pretty!"

William lowers his head, raises his eyes and smiles. "You like it?" he asks.

"No," Kelly says.

"No," William says, his smile fading.

"I don't like it, I LOVE IT!" Kelly grabs William and tickles him. William laughs , Kelly kisses him on his soft round cheek, they both fall on the floor.

"I'm sorry I pushed you earlier," Kelly says. "Are you okay?"

"Yeah, I'm pretty tough," William says.

Kelly kisses William's forehead and gives him another hug.

"I love you," she says.

"I know," William smiles goofily.

Kelly calls Kristen.

Kristen: Yes bitch?

Kelly: I can go.

Kristen: You are shitting me! Nice! Pick me up now!

Kelly: In an hour.

Kristen: Bullshit! I want to get there early so I can get a buzz before Mike Donovan comes.

Kelly: I'll try to make it 45 minutes.

Kristen: Steal some liquor from your parents.

Kelly: No way! I don't even drink.

Kristen: Whatever you prude bitch. Just get here in 30.

Kelly: I'll try.

Kristen: Byyyyeee

Kelly enters the family room. Her father is watching a baseball game with a beer in his hand. His face is still dirty from the garden. She sits on the edge of the couch and squeezes the purse in her hands. Her father swigs his beer and looks at her.

"I'm sorry," Kelly says, her eyes on her father's feet.

"For what?" her father asks.

Kelly rolls her eyes and shakes her leg up and down.

"For being a bi… for being disrespectful."

Kelly's father finishes his beer and wants to say more. He begins a couple times but stops.

"Do you mean that or is it because your Mom bribed you with be able to go shopping with your friend?

"A little of both," Kelly smiles. Her Dad shakes his head and smirks.

"I admire your honesty," he says before swigging his beer. "I accept your apology."

"Cool," Kelly says.

"Give me a hug and then you can run off into the world."

Kelly gives her Dad a big hug, he kisses her on the cheek.

"I love you," he says.

"I lo-" Kelly's iPhone beeps and she pulls from her father's embrace and checks it.

A text message from Kristen: *kiss his ass yet????*

"Can I go to the mall with Kristen now?" Kelly asks her father.

Her father looks at her and puts the beer down.

"Yes, but you were saying something before you got distracted by your fancy phone."

"Hugh?"

"You were saying something to me, weren't you?"

"I love you?"

"Yes, I think so."

"Oh yeah, totally Dad. Duh, like you know that."

"Well it's nice to hear once in a while," he says before finishing his beer.

"You are like so melodramatic sometimes Dad," Kelly says with a teasing laughter.

"Touché," he smiles, his eyes back on the baseball game.

Kelly texts Kristen back: *on my way slut!*

"Bye Daddy, I totally love you Daddy," Kelly giggles playfully as she grabs her keys and runs out of the house.

Kelly pulls up to Kristen's Mom's apartment and Kirsten is sitting on the front steps smoking a cigarette. Kristen slides in the car. She has a sprite bottle with a red liquid in it.

"Hey bitch, took you long enough. Want some?" Kristen says.

Kelly grabs the sprite bottle and smells it. "What the hell is that? Vodka?"

"Yuppers," Kristen laughs. "Need to get my swerve on a little before the par-tay."

Kelly hand the bottle back and Kristen takes a swig. She makes a painful face when she is done.

"Tastes nasty, hugh?" Kelly asks.

"Hell yeah it tastes nasty. I error'd on the side of vodka vs. cranberry. Sure you don't want a little?"

"No way. I need to drive, remember?"

"Shit, we'd get there faster of you drank this. You are like *such* a prude driver!"

"Prude and alive," Kelly says.

"What-ev," Kristen says as she rummages through her purse. "Wanna smoke a jizzoint?" she asks, showing Kelly what looks like a small white wrinkled cigarette.

"A what?" Kelly asks.

"A doobie. A spliff. A joint. A Marley masterpiece!"

"Weed?"

"Yes bitch, *weeeed*."

"No thanks. And don't smoke that in my car. My parents would kill me."

"No worries, choir girl. I'm saving this for Mike Donovan. We'll smoke it after we have sex."

"You are nasty."

"Totally joking, choir girl. Or am I?" Kristen laughs , then takes another swig out of the Sprite bottle, followed by another cough and grimace.

"Whatever."

"What-ev-er."

The house where the party is belongs to the uncle of Trevor Cleegler, a former student of Kelly's high school. He was expelled earlier in the year for selling marijuana in the quad. They found $700 and half a pound of weed in his gym locker.

The house is huge. It has a long driveway under a white stucco arch. The quarter mile driveway curves 120 degrees into a four car garage. Mammoth trees litter the front yard and four Mexican landscapers are feeding large dead branches into a chipper machine that growls and grinds, turning the tree limbs into wood chips.

Kelly parks on the street, cars already filling the driveway and several on the street.

"Hold on bitch – don't get out yet," Kristen says. "How do I look?" Kristen pulls her red skirt up, then it pushes down. She pushes her breasts up, cleavage popping out of her blouse, then winks at Kelly. "Fuckable?"

Kelly looks at Kristen and shakes her head "no".

"Fuuuuck you, slut! I do to! I look fuckable, doable, eatable, lickable, spankable –"

"Date-rape-able."

"Oh no you didn't!" Kristen screams. "Shit, you probably *would* date-rate me you lesbo!"

"No worries," Kelly says, "I'm going after Kyle tonight."

"Kyle? Kyle Sampson? That fucking dwarf?"

"No," Kelly laughs, a little offended, "Kyle Kinks."

"Kinky Kyle Kinks? Kinky Kyle 'I actually like to eat a girl out' Kinks? Damn bitch, I didn't know you were so horny!"

Kelly laughs loudly, sort of snorts. "I'm only kidding!" she says. "I can't believe you actually think I would get with Kinky Kyle Kinks!"

Kristen hits Kelly. "You are stupid. Besides, he wouldn't be at this party. He's not in with the senior crowd like us."

"Like you," Kelly says.

"You'll be cool like me someday, don't sweat. Just follow my lead and let a few guys pinch your little sophomore booty tonight."

"Whatever," Kelly says, rolling her eyes.

"What-ev-er!"

Kristen finished the sprite bottle and smiles at Kelly. "Let's par-tay!" she screams into the quiet neighborhood.

Kelly and Kristen walk to the back yard and find small crowd congregating around a large pool.

Kristen screams, "Kevin! Kevin! Hey you fag, what are you doing here?"

Kevin walks up and hugs Kristen.

"I heard there were some dirty sweaty Mexican dudes working here so I came right over," he says.

Kristen laughs, hits Kevin across the chest, tells him he is hilarious.

"You gonna get as wild as you did last party?" Kevin asks, winking at Kristen as he swigs his beer.

"What-ev! I like don't even remember that lame party," Kristen says with a flirtatious smile.

"Oh that's a shame. I was hoping for a repeat performance."

"You need to simmer your boil, big boy. Find me some booze and maybe my evil twin will return. No guarantees though," Kristen says with a smirk.

"Follow me," Kevin says. "I will take you to the promise land."

Kevin pinches Kristen's backside, she giggles, calls him *bad*, then follows him inside.

Kelly hurries to catch up with Kristen.

"Like what happened at the last party?" Kelly asks.

"Nothing," Kristen says, distracted, scanning the party.

"Didn't sound like nothing," Kelly says.

"Whatev prude bitch," Kristen sort of snaps. "Hey, go get us a table and I'll meet you there after I snag a drink."

"Whatever," Kelly says, turning around and heading back towards the pool.

Kelly takes a seat at a table in the corner, across from a hippy looking boy who is smoking a joint.

Kelly pulls out her iPhone and tweets: *Why am I at this party? My friend??? Kristen already ditched me.*

"Want some?" the blonde hippy with loose dreadlocks asks, extending the joint.

"No thank you," Kelly smiles. "I'm like totally stoned already," she says rolling her eyes.

"Right on," he smiles with his eyes closed.

Kelly tweets: *Wonder what weed is like. people look so dumb but also happy.*

"I'd totally make out with you," dreadlock blonde says while staring at his joint.

Kelly tweets: *stoner dude wants to make out with his joint. so freakin weird!*

"Do you want to make out with me?"

Kelly looks up from her iPhone and sees the stoner dude is talking to her, not his joint.

"Excuse me?" she says.

"You ever had sex on mushrooms?" he asks, watching with fascination a snake of smoke ascending through the air.
Kelly rolls her eyes and looks away.

"It's fucking wicked," he says. "Although it can be difficult if you start laughing too hard. It's mind blowing how many things you notice on shrooms and how *fucking funny* those things are."

"I'm sure," Kelly musters before burying her head in her iPhone.

Kelly tweets: *get me out of here like Yesterday. OMG this guy is totally psycho!*

Blonde stoner laughs and leans forwards towards Kelly.

"Hey," he says softly, his lazy green eyes focused on Kelly. "Don't think you are better than me because you smell good, don't drink, never get high, and actually do your homework. Life is purely random and you may be cleaning my million dollar urine off a toilet seat someday. Or worse."

Blonde stoner then tokes his joint and starts laughing.

Kelly turns red and text tweets: *whatta asshole!*

"Totally fucking with you," stoner blonde laughs as he coughs on a toke. "Totally joking baby girl. Keep it pure and keep it straight if that's you. It's the safer path."

Stoner stands up and takes one last toke, exhales, and says "although safe and pure *is* boring and tense as fuck if you ask me." He walks away.

Kelly tweets: *and why ami here again? Total losers!! Wanna leave!*

Kristen walks back onto the patio in a bikini top, her large breasts busting out, her red eyes glazed, a can of beer in her hand. Mike Donovan has his hand on her backside and she is laughing.

"Hey bitch," she says to Kelly as she walks by. Mike Donovan looks at Kelly and winks, then slaps Kristen on the butt before pushing her in the pool.

Kelly eyes the keg, then tweets: *maybe I shld drink. Party wld b more fun. Btw…Kristen is totlly NOT a reel frend.*

The Top 100 thumps through a sound system and the pool is filled with screaming, shrieking and laughing teens. Red cups are everywhere – on the ledge of the pool, in hands elevated above the water, and floating empty in the pool. Kelly knows no one and recognizes only a few from school. The day is beginning to fade into night and Kristen has disappeared into the house with Mike Donovan and Kevin, the guy Kelly met when they first arrived.

Kelly tweets: *I am NOT waiting for Kristen all nite. Drunk people are dumb.*

Kelly tweets: *seniors r totl losers. Girls r totl sluts. Maybe I shld just leave.*

Two boys wearing the same Abercrombie shirts with the same hair style sit down at the table across from Kelly and are laughing.

"I've got another one for you," Abercrombie #1 says. "Have you ever seen a black person on the Jetsons?"

Laughing, Abercrombie #2 says, "Hell no."

"Then the future looks good!" Abercrombie #1 and #2 laugh loudly and fist bump each other.

"That one was dope!"

"For shizzie!"

"Here's one for you," Abercrombie #2 says. "What do you say to a black person in a three-piece suit?"

"What?"

Abercrombie #2 finishes his Bud Light, belches loudly and laughs, "Will the defendant please rise!"

Big laughter, fist bumps.

The stereo is blasting Lil Wayne's new song .

"Awwww shit, this tune is dope as hell! Abercrombie #1 says.

"Hell yeah, bro. Lil Wayne is the shit!" Abercrombie #2 says.

"We need to find some pussy tonight," Abercrombie #1 says.

Abercrombie #2 nods his head 'yes' and looks over at Kelly. "What's your name, girl?" he says.

Kelly looks up from her iPhone where she has just tweeted: *two frat boys just sat down. Look the same. Totally racist.*

"Excuse me?" she says.

"Your name, what is it?" Abercrombie #2 says.

"Kelly," she says.

"Cool," he says. "You look kinda young for this party, which is cool. Age ain't no thing with me."

Kelly rolls her eyes, tell them she is 13. Abercrombie #1 excuses himself quickly, somewhat embarrassed. Abercrombie #2 stays a moment longer, as if pondering Kelly's age. His buddy grabs him, calls him a perve. They both walk off.

Kelly is alone at the table.

She tweets: *what losers! I'm gonna leave. Kristen is probly havn sex with evry guy!*

Kelly's phone rings. It is her Mom. She sends the call to voicemail.

Kelly texts her Mom: *sorry mom, at mall busy trying on a dress. Will call u later.*

Kelly's Mom texts: *It is 7:30. Your curfew is 9:00.*

Kelly texts: *I know my lame curfew thank you. Going to Kristen's for a few. Be home after.*

Mom texts: *call me when u get there.*

Kelly texts: *ok*

A boy sits at the table with Kristen. He is short with brown hair, round eyes, a single dimple. He is texting on his phone and laughing. He looks up and smiles at Kelly, then looks back down at his phone and texts a short message, starts laughing again.

Kelly takes her iPhone off the table and tweets: *total hotty just sat down. smiled at me :)*

The brown haired boy puts his phone in his pocket, lights a cigarette. "Hey," he smiles through the smoke and the thumping of Black Eyed Peas.

"Hey," Kelly says.

He swigs his bottle of beer and takes another drag, leans back in his chair and scans the party.

Kelly tweets: *OMG guy sittn across from me is soooo cute! Just said hey to me*

"Black Eyed Peas get a little old," the brown haired boy says. "All their songs sound alike."

"I totally agree," Kelly says quickly.

"Yeah, I mean like what the fuck is original these days anyway? Even Coldplay have turned into whores."

"Yup, yeah, I agree, definitely," Kelly says.

Brown haired boy is wearing old worn jeans, a brown t-shirt that says "flawed at the core" and his short brown hair is disheveled.

"My name's Colin," he says.

"Mine's Kelly," she says.

"Cool," Colin says as he swigs his beer.

Kelly tweets: *just met Colin. Sooooo cute...OMG did I say that already?*

"You're on that phone a lot. Must have a lot of friends."

"I have a few," Kelly says.

"I don't," Colin says. "I know a lot of people but I don't have a lot of friends. Just one really. Maybe two."

Kelly rubs her phone, shakes her leg up and down, glances at Colin, he is looking at her. She looks away quickly towards the crowd.

"Who really loves you?" Colin says.

"Excuse me?" Kelly asks.

"Not you," he says. "People in general. Who really loves you? That is the test of a real friend. The rest are a bunch of self-serving parasites." Colin is smiling at Kelly and then starts laughing. "Sorry," he says, "that might be a little heavy for a first impression."

"It's cool," Kelly says. "You're deep. That's so cool. Not a lot of people are deep."

"You're cute," Colin says. Kelly blushes.

"I'm serious, you are." he says.

"Thank you," Kelly smiles.

"So who does really love you? Anyone here?"

Kelly looks around and laughs. "No way. I barely know anyone here except my friend Kristen."

"Where is she?"

"Drunk somewhere probably having sex."

"Nice," Colin smiles. "Let me guess – you drove."

Kelly nods affirmative.

"Friend, eh? Sounds more like a parasite."

"Well, I guess not a friend by *your* definition," Kelly says. "Maybe not by mine either. She's a new friend I guess."

Colin drops his cigarette to the floor and steps on it. "So back to the question," he says, "who loves you?"

Kelly rubs her phone, suddenly wants a swig of beer even though she hates the taste of it.

"My family I guess," she eventually says.

"The obligatory love where they are somewhat detached from your life or something really thoughtful and unconditional?

"I don't know," she says.

"The sort of love where you could tell them anything and not worry about their reaction?"

Kelly shifts in her seat, runs her hand through her hair, rolls her eyes into the sky, sighs.

"I don't know," Kelly says again with a nervous giggle.

"Sure you do," Colin says without patience.

"Are you always so intense?"

"Just real," Colin half smiles.

Kelly sighs. Twirls her hair in her fingers.

"Yes, I guess so," she finally says. "Yeah, they love me like that, you know, like unconditional. I mean, I have never really thought about it though."

"Wow," Colin says, sitting back, beer against his chest. "You're a lucky girl."

"Well, I mean they aren't like perfect or anything. They are totally in my business all the time and don't trust me."

"How old are you?" Colin asks.

"Does it matter?" Kelly asks weakly.

"I don't know," Colin says.

"I'm sixteen," Kelly says. "How old are you?"

"27," Colin says.

"Really!?"

"No, not really," Colin says. "I'm eighteen."

"You're stupid," Kelly laughs.

"I know."

Colin looks at his empty beer, Kelly watches him with a smile. Colin looks up at Kelly and Kelly looks away.

"I'm gonna grab another beer. Want something?"

"Oh no, I'm totally fine thanks."

Colin disappears into the chaos of the party.

Kelly takes a deep breath and exhales slowly. Justin Bieber's new song "Baby" starts playing and Kelly takes a deep breath and smiles.

She tweets: *what does luv feel like?*

She tweets: *I feel some weird energy. Feel great. Feel nervous but a good kind. Crazy!*

She tweets: *his name is colin. Did I say that? So hot! So deep! So cool! 18 yrs old, OMG is that too old???*

She tweets: *does colin have a gf? Should I ask? OMG I am freakin out!!! :) :) :) !!!!*

Kelly's phone rings. It's her Dad. She sends him to voicemail, looks at the time: 9:15.

"Shit!" she panics.

Kelly texts Dad: *on way home, stopped for gas.*

Dad texts back: *ok honey. Be safe. We love you.*

"Everything okay?" Colin says, standing over Kelly with two beers in his hand.

"I'm late," she says. "I need to find Kristen like now and get home."

"It's only nine," Colin says swigging his beer.

"Tell me something I don't know," she says.

"Tell them you're sleeping over at your friends." Colin extends a beer to Kelly. "I got you a beer. Let's hang out."

"I don't drink and I need to get home," Kelly says, scanning the party for Kristen.

"My parents are out of town," Colin says. "Just chill with me tonight," he says, lighting a cigarette.

"What's your number," Kelly says. "I'll call you later."

Colin and Kelly exchange numbers. Colin gives Kelly a quick kiss on the lips and Kelly smiles, wants to tweet: *colin just kissed me, omg it was amazing!*

"You should sneak out tonight," Colin says into Kelly's ear, his arm around her waist. "I can pick you up and we can just go for a drive or something."

Kelly moves close to Colin, kisses him softly on the lips, says "Ok text me a little later."

"You got it girl," Colin says with a wink.

Kelly's phone rings. It's her Mom. She sends it to voicemail.

"Okay Colin, I have to go. Don't forget to text me."

"I won't," Colin says as he rubs Kelly's backside.

"You are *bad*," Kelly giggles before running into the house to look for Kristen.

Kelly walks quickly through the house for several minutes looking for Kristen. There's lots of screaming conversations and laughter, lots of beer bottles and liquor cups, cigarettes burning in every hand, smoke hovering throughout.

Kelly runs into the basement calling Kristen's name, asking people if they have seen her.

"Kristen who?" they say.

Kelly opens the door to a bedroom and the two Abercrombie guys are with a blonde girl who is bending over the sink with a dollar bill in her nose. One of them has a hand on her backside, the other sees Kelly and smiles lustfully. Kelly slams the door shut and runs into the rear of the basement. She hears what sounds like a helium tank, sees people with balloons to their mouths. They look like zombies.

Almost a half hour into her frantic search, Kelly bursts into an upstairs bathroom and finds Kristen naked on the floor with two guys standing over her, erections in hand. One is Mike Donovan, the other Kevin.

" Oh my God!" Kelly screams. "What are you doing!?"

Kristen sits up and screams, "Bitch get the fuck out!"

"But Kristen-"

"Get out!" Kristen shrieks.

"Do you know what you're doing?"

The boys are drunk, laughing. They ask Kelly to join them.

"Get the fuck out you prude fucking bitch!" Kristen screams.

Kelly slams the door, runs down the stairs and out of the house. She is crying.

There are dozens of cars lining the street. Kelly finds her car quickly and starts the engine. The clock reads: 10:00. As she is driving off, her phone rings. She looks down and sees it's her Mom.   She sends it to voicemail, looks up, sees a stop sign and slams on breaks. One handed, Kelly texts her Mom: *jesus I'm on way! Relax! Tryn to drive!!!!* Kelly turns left on Hampton Drive. There's a red pick-up truck in front of her. The phone rings again. Kelly looks down and it's her Dad calling. She lets off the gas and texts her Dad: *20 minutes away. Had bad nite. Pleez stop calln. Tryn to drive.*

Kelly tosses her phone onto the passenger seat, takes a right on Randolph Street and comes to a stop light. The light turns green and Kelly turns left on Thompson Avenue, gets in the right lane and enters the onramp to the expressway.   There is a slow Honda Civic in front of her. The phone rings and Kelly looks down towards the passenger seat. She grabs the phone, glances up at the Honda Civic in front of her, down at the phone in her hand. It's Kristen.

"Hello," Kelly answers.

"Where are you? Where did you go? I need to go home!"

"I had to leave," Kelly says, merging onto the expressway, then speeding up to pass the Honda Civic. "It's way past my curfew and my parents are pissed."

"You left!? You fucking left me here!?"

Kelly passes the Honda and slows to merge back into the right lane.

"I tried to get you but you totally yelled at me," Kelly says, whining.

"I'm fucking drunk you stupid bitch! Come back here and get me!"

Kelly notices a police officer behind her, slows down. She glances at the road ahead, back at the rearview mirror, then at the road ahead.

"I can't," she tells Kristen. "I am almost home and my parents are totally pissed."

"You fucking loser get back here NOW and pick me up!. You are my ride remember!?"

Kelly checks her speed – 53 MPH – returns eyes to the road. "Have Mike Donovan fucking drive you," Kelly says with more assertion. "And stop calling me a bitch you BITCH!" Kelly pulls her phone from her ear to her lap, looks down and hits the END button. When she looks up she is veering onto the shoulder. "Shit!" she cries as she corrects her steering and glances with rising panic into the rearview mirror. The cop is gone.

Kelly exits the expressway on Willow East. She grabs her phone and texts her Mom -*5 min awy*- before turning left onto Forest Way Drive. Her text indicator beeps and glancing down, she sees a message waiting from Colin. The song "Baby" by Justin Bieber comes on the radio and Kelly turns it up, sings along, her smile wide, her energy alive and wild. She turns her brights on to illuminate the dark road and the edge of the dense forest. She looks down at Colin's text:

u r beautiful, want to see u again tonite!

Kelly lets off the gas, widens her smile, and texts Colin:

u r hot. Wnt bdly to c u soo-

A fawn appears in the middle of the road and Kelly looks up. She drops her phone and grabs the steering wheel with both hands while slamming on the breaks. Now skidding, Kelly jerks the steering wheel left to avoid colliding with the fawn and the car begins to spin. A guard rail appears ahead, the car spinning in its direction. Kelly closes her eyes and braces for impact as the rear of the car crashes into the open end of the guard rail. The heavy steel edge of the rail then skewers the car in rapid succession: through the trunk, the back seat, the driver's seat, Kelly's body, the steering wheel, the dashboard and into the engine.

The car is still. The night is calm. The engine is dead but hissing. One headlight shoots across the road and illuminates the fawn faintly twitching in the street, its mother now nudging her. Kelly opens her eyes and sees her right arm with pink bracelet impaled into the dashboard. She looks down and sees her stomach half gone, her right leg severed.

Her cell phone starts ringing. Kelly whispers without volume or movement, *"Daddy... please help me."*

The fawn stops moving, its mother trots back into the dark forest, and three sounds permeate the dark night: the hissing engine, restless crickets and the ceaseless ringing and beeping of Kelly's iPhone.

The Color of Love and Batteries

I sit here and get high and have a glass of wine by myself on a Friday night and I contemplate whether or not I want to go out and kick it with some guys from work. They are white. I am not. I'm not sure exactly why I decided to smoke half a joint and drink some wine. I suppose it has something to do with fear. That's what most would say. I say it has more to do with mood. I'm just trying to put myself into the right mood for this evening. People are always doing crazy things to put themselves in the right mood for their special little social engagements; maybe a club, maybe a dinner, a date... Just think about it... What they wear, who they go with, what they drive, what their story is, how they smell, how much they weigh, how tan they are, how much money they may have... I get high and drink a little wine. That's not to say I don't also do all of those things I mentioned (except tan, of course), my point is that we're all fucking crazy and insecure and subjected to the same social pressures... Why is my getting a little high making me any less valuable than the person who isn't getting high when that person is probably more stressed, more tense, more confused, more insecure, etcetera, etcetera than I am. I smoke a little weed and have a little wine and I am able to alter my perception in such a way that I can alleviate myself from much of the madness I would normally be baring the burden of... I in fact become much more honest with who I am exactly and who other people are... so how is that a bad thing? Sounds like I'm rationalizing my substance abuse, doesn't it? Fuck it, it ain't abuse, it's purposeful use...

My mind is racing and my emotions are gaining momentum... So much to think about but there is one thing that has been on my mind for some time... me and my struggle with going out, meeting guys (or guy), dealing with the bullshit, playing the game, taking risks, playing pretend, leading guys on, taking guys in...

I can't seem to get it right. I know who I want to be and I know who I feel comfortable being, but sometimes people or circumstances ignite a flame inside me that flickers a little more wild than I would like. I can be so calm and sure of myself one moment, you know, like grounded and mature, and then all of a sudden my mind begins to speed up and zig zag in various directions and a different me begins to take over. Suddenly I want people to pay attention to me, I want the cool guys or the attractive guys to take notice of me. I want to be the center of it all. I want this but I'm not entirely sure I can handle it. I constantly tell myself that I am in control, that this is what I want, that's it's all good, ya know, fun times. But in reality I'm a little scared. And lonely. Wherever the night may take me, I'm in constant search for confirmation of my beauty or coolness or popularity. I want the cute guys to cater to me, the cool guys to acknowledge me as one of them, to flirt with me, and I want the deep and intellectual guys to speak to me, you know, like on that level. But when the night ends and I return to my apartment alone, maybe I kissed someone, maybe I didn't, maybe I handed out and received digits, maybe I didn't... I return to my solitude not so convinced my evening was a success. No matter what kind of fly time I had, a lingering sadness weighs me down. I begin asking questions that are important and relevant but many times I wish would not rise up into my mind. Questions like: Who am I really? Who did I meet tonight that I could truly trust? Who really has the potential to understand, respect and potentially adore my world, my past, my vision of the future?

Drinking my wine and listening to Sade and getting a little higher than I intended (this always seems to happen), I can't help but focus on love. When I think about love, I think about a man, and when I think about that man, I think about the color of me. Is this a problem? Am I close-minded to think exclusively about a black man coming out of the shadows of life and being my Mr. Wonderful? Do I even want a Mr. Wonderful right now? Sounds cheesy, lame, boring... Mr. Wonderful might be too nice, or too thoughtful, or even *too* good looking... Yes, a man can be too attractive for me. There's always something a little off about the guys who strike me immediately as really really attractive. Either they're gay, ego maniacs, crazy, or their penises are hung like a can of tuna. Motion in the ocean? *Please.* That's what the *tongue*'s for. I suppose it's some joke God has played on me, or rather it is one of God's subtle blessings or messages that keep me on the lookout for more depth, something more valuable and satisfying than a nice hard body, strong cheekbones and a firm round ass I could squeeze and pull and squeeze and pull...all...night....long....

Sex is cool and security is beautiful. I've been fucked with, I've been lied to, I've been cheated on, I've been manipulated, I've been broken... I'm getting too old for that shit. Sex ain't *that* great to go through madness for an entire lifetime. Maybe sex needs to become secondary to security. But why would I want a guy who makes me secure, you know, emotionally, but he can't hit the spot? The *spot*, gentlemen. The *spot*! Hit it or quit it... Wouldn't I get bored? Wouldn't my settling for security only lead me down a path of discontent? And who the fuck wants to be discontent in life? Boredom and fantasy and irritation begin to rule the day, the mind, the sexual drive. Mr. Wonderful may be a sweetheart and buy me cute little gifts, maybe say sweet things, dress nice, be responsible, hold me in the morning...but that lame-ass 'good guy' ain't making me feel like a sexual beast, and shit, I *am* a sexual beast. Well, I *can* be. I love some good sex, some sweet cock, a strong tongue, my ass in the air and my face in the pillow and a sting on my ass from the relentless spanking I beg to endure. It's not like I'm a *ho*. Any female who denies these very cravings is a flat out liar, either that, or they just haven't had it, been through it, experienced it, you know... the cock and tongue rollercoaster ride that every female wishes would never end. Never.

I've got needs. Shit. Standards too. Somehow those needs and standards need to meet in a happy place and deliver me my man. Like I said, when I dream about this man, he's always the color of me. But tonight I'm going out with a bunch of white guys. White guys. I can't say I'm very optimistic about this either. Whenever I socialize with white guys, especially if there is alcohol involved, there's always a guarantee of some real fucking ignorance. Not the racist kind, but rather the stupid shit- me being some sort of novelty to their inexperienced white minds. You know, them assuming I listen to a certain kind of *black* music, or that I can dance like the booty ho video chics on BET, or that I can tell them what exactly soul food is cause they've always been curious, or the way I talk, my *urban* accent, my *black speak,* like 'marinate' or 'been done that' or *"You feel me?"*... and they start saying these things, mimicking me I suppose, an envious mimic, wishing they sounded as smooth and cool as I do, as *black people* do, forcing the words out with uncomfortable smiles or sarcasm that makes me never want to say those words again. Back up off my culture, white boy! You're making it lame! -I never say this but I sure as hell want to some times. Are they ignorant? Maybe ignorance is too harsh a word, but they are definitely special, naïve, annoying as all hell when I think about it. So why would I want to go out with them? I don't know. I don't have shit else to do. Love though? Tonight? White guys? Not likely. Like I just said, I don't have shit else to do.

Being a black female I experience a very unique perspective on American life. And this perspective is very much mis-understood or not even acknowledged by the rest of non-black America. Sure I do meet cute and funny and smart white guys, but it saddens me when I consider their naivety and ignorance to the world that is all I know and feel. I'm not looking for pity. Nor do I expect a guy to know and understand

everything about me. That's not what I'm preaching. But he should
have the ability to understand and internalize the fundamentals of being a
black person and a black female in the United States of America. I
suppose this is about a guy having the ability to step inside me, to love
me in a way that he begins to feel and see what I see from the sometimes
insecure, at times paranoid perspective of being a black female in white
America. I'm not stupid, I know many white guys think of me as
nothing more than a 'hot black chic', maybe a potential exotic fuck,
something they could tell their friends about to feed their own egos, their
insatiable quest towards sexual accomplishment.

"Yeah dude, I totally fucked a black chic."

"Really? Fucking wild, dude. Is it true they are a wild fuck?"

"Totally"

"Must be the African blood or some shit."

Laughter and high fives....

Not that every white guy is like this. Many mean well but just won't
ever get it. I just couldn't trust them to be consistent, confident and
loyal... Bless their hearts, but I just can't be with a man who hasn't
reached a certain level. Not that black guys are the answer either. There
exists a whole dynamic of various types of black guys out there that I
won't even get into. So many of them fail to satisfy me as well. Most of
them love to convey a persona of concrete confidence or slick and
slippery coolness, but let me tell you a little secret, they are just as
insecure as the rest of us, sometimes more. But I know why, you see, I
can look deeper than the surface before I judge a man. Being black in
America is a really insecure experience. We were told for so long we
were weak and insufficient and second class (even no class!) that it
became a necessity for psychological survival to develop thick skin, not
to reveal to others how scared we sometimes were and are. I love my
people. I love my people for all their strengths and all their fears and
weaknesses, cause you know what, we share a common history that will
always unite us by the fabric of its sheer madness and horror. Our
American history is nothing like white American history. And
sometimes I think white people don't fully comprehend what that means.
Not that I'm living my life looking back on that and feeling sorry for
myself or my people, but I'm sure as hell not going to forget it or
marginalize it like many people in America do.

"It's the past, we've come a long way, racism is over, slavery is long
gone, bla bla bla..." Many white people actually think and believe this,
bless their narrow little hearts and minds.

I know I'm making it sound like I think my people, black people and
black woman, are so complicated and wronged that nobody but us could

ever understand or relate to or love us. That's not my intention. I don't really believe that. Well sometimes I do, but I know it's not the case. It's just that I haven't met many non-black folks that I can honestly say really *get it*. Especially any white dudes. And as I have already mentioned, the only guys who really turn me on when I look at them are black men.

No white guy has ever affected me like that, you know, given me reason to fantasize about him. I think they're interesting, I mean some are cute, but they just don't have that oomph, that zip, that zap, that flash, that edge, that fire, that shock, that charge that electrifies my shit, rattles my shit, shakes it all up and makes me craving some of whatever he's got. No white guy has ever done that. They are either not that cool, nice but not cool, cool but not that cool, or they think they are cool but they ain't. They think they're being real, but they ain't. They think they're being slick but they're as rough as some broken concrete. It is rare, real real rare, to find a white guy who can chill with some real fine black females and be real, be calm, be smooth, be confident, be himself, be different, interesting, stimulating... Maybe I'm prejudice. Or biased. I think I'm just being honest. I want a real man. A man who makes me think. Makes me want to be around him. To hear the words that come out of his mouth. A man who can challenge the way I think. A man who not only wants to understand me, but does understand me. And I'm not so sure that man exists, really. It's hard enough to find a guy who even *wants* to understand my world. He's too busy spinning around in his. I mean, guys are cool and all, but damn, they just don't get it. It's the little things. It's the deeper things. Yeah you can fuck my brains out and I'll definitely enjoy that shit, but that doesn't mean I want to spend time with you. The problem with getting your brains fucked out is that it's like eating McDonald's—you love it when it's happening, but it leaves you feeling empty, kind of nauseous, and wanting something much more fulfilling.

Could a white guy ever appreciate the depth of my beauty? Could he ever stop seeing black and start loving brown? Could he ever stop seeing black? Black. That's the question. Will he love these eyes as my eyes? These big eyes with their beautiful black pupils set in an immaculate sea of white? Would he move above these eyes and rub his fingers over my threaded black brows and down the smooth bridge of my nose, leaning close and pressing his lips upon its rounded tip? Could he admire the shape of my nose, the way it spreads gracefully to the cheek lines that curve like a piece of art around my adorable lips, lips that are the highlight of my gorgeous smile?
Would you?

Would you skim your lips across my nose and over my shut eyes....kiss my eyelids....rub your cheek across my cheek.... nibble on my ear lobe (the spot that gets me hot!)... Breathe gently on my brown neck as you smell my brown skin, kiss that skin, rub your soft fingers all over that skin, across the back of my neck and down the arch of my back... pressing your body against my body, feel my temperature, my heat, my heart and it's quickening beat....holding my soft face in your hands as you work your lips down my neck... and kiss my chest... above the breasts... working your way down...slowly...slowly...like you mean it and you love it and you never want to let it go.... Never rushing it...holding me tight, looking into my eyes, sliding the back of your fingers across my cheek and telling me I'm just *so* beautiful, the *most* beautiful, like an African queen or a goddess or a princess..... making me feel as special as I've always dreamt of feeling, the way I tell myself to feel but sometimes find it hard to believe... giving me that pleasure, that treasure...

Touch my brown chest, caress my sensitive breasts, kiss me gently, around the nipple and over the nipple and nibble on that nipple, lick that nipple, love that brown nipple as much as you love me.... Move your hands down, slide them across the round cheeks of my ass and push your body up against mine. Hold me, press your excitement up against mine and slide those fingers to the front, to the front, lower... can you feel how wet I am? That's you baby, that's my love for you. Ain't just any guy who can get me like that. You can. You know why? Cause you mean it. You love it. You love it so much you take it slow...until I start loving it so much I tell you to speed that shit up and you can only smile as you slip a couple fingers up inside me. Damn, that shit feels *sooo* good, baby.

Push me down on the couch, baby. Push me down and pull your pants off, quickly! Can't you see how desperate I am for your love? Get down here on top of me, lay that warm body of yours on mine, kiss me, and fuck me... you don't have to be gentle, just fuck me cause I know you love me, you don't need to prove that shit any more, just fuck me hard cause I need that shit, I need to be fucked hard by love, fuck me hard with your love, baby, cause I ain't ever had that. Never. I'm sorry baby... if I'd known you were coming I would never have fucked anyone, I can promise you that..... I mean I've been fucked with lust, fucked with fear, fucked with hate, fucked with motives, fucked with lies... baby it seems I've been fucked with every fucking thing but love. And I need that love, baby. I want that love so deep inside me it hurts, baby, cause I've been hurt so much I need to be hurt by love... I can't explain it... please just slide that beautiful cock inside me and don't stop until I can't take it no more... fuck me with love... Oh baby, where you going? You going down there? Shit baby, you don't need to do that for me, really, it's cool, you can just skip to the fucking, I promise, oh baby baby baby baby baby... damn! your tongue feels good... oh baby, keep your tongue right there, that's the fucking spot, yes baby, yes yes yes yes, oh just suck on it baby, suck on it, that's it baby, that's it, damn you are good at this, yes! stick those fingers inside me, yes! suck on that clit, massage that clit... keep finger fucking me deep, oh baby! Can you feel that juice??? I ain't ever felt this good. You love me, this is love, this is being in love, making love, sharing love, thank you baby thank you.... please stick it in me, please! Please! I need your cock now, I can't take it, I'm greedy I know, but I already told you I'm desperate, I need to be fucked by you baby... you... cause I love you so much....oh baby I'm sorry I'm crying, please don't pay no attention to my tears, those tears aren't today's tears, those are yesterday's tears and they've got to go cause love has arrived and all that misery and loneliness and sadness ain't got no place no more.... just put your love inside me and I promise those tears will disappear-

The buzz goes in and out... and before I know it, the sensation, the fantasy, the love, the fuck, the batteries are all dead...

I take a hit from the joint, pour some more wine, drink that wine, and turn Sade up on my stereo. Damn I'm warm. I can feel the sweat rolling slowly down my spine. I stand and walk in front of the mirror and look at my body. I'm not even sure a white dude could handle this shit. I'm black and beautiful, as they say. My thighs are strong, my curves are long, my ass is round and firm. My tits could be a little firmer, but shit, they are nice just the same. I love my nipples; not too big, not too small, just perfect. I love it how my brown cheeks just glow when I smile. My skin, damn my skin is alive and healthy. I'm only 25 and I'll be looking like this when I'm 55. Ya gotta love the longevity of the black female. But these aren't the things I want a man to love. Well not entirely. What is going to make me feel special is his attention to my less obvious attributes, like my eyes, my nose, my toes or my fingers, my ears or my neck, the less obvious and largely ignored attributes of a woman that men fail to acknowledge because they are just so damn simple minded. I want a man who's got the depth, the perception, the appreciation for everything on my body, a man who can look at my chewed up fingernails and tell me how cute and adorable they are, because they are mine, they are a part of me and he just absolutely adores the being that is me. A man who can find beauty in me when I'm at my most ugly...a man who can hold me when I'm most scared, who can calm me when I'm most rattled , bring clarity when I'm most confused, please me when I'm most horny, make me laugh when I'm most depressed... I don't want no ordinary love, I want a love that strikes and strums and strokes a chord so deep inside me I'd be terrified of living a day without him and his love for me. Oh I know I sound really selfish, but I wouldn't accept this adoration from any man. Only from a man I equally adored. And what are the odds of that??? People say they are in love, they even marry and have children, but you just know that there exists something deeper, something more real, more intense than what they have. I don't want to settle. That's like quitting, that's weak and pointless. You are a failure if you refuse to keep searching.

I listen to Sade and I can feel the emotion but I have no one to feel that emotion for. I listen to Cherish the Day and Kiss of Life and I feel the love, but it's like I'm loving a mystery, a phantom, a maybe... not a definite. I can't live my life dreaming... I need the reality....

Maybe I'm too deep and intense. Maybe it's a curse to want too much out of a man. Maybe I'd be better off if I was content with playing around, fucking whomever, skating on the surface of life without this internal pressure to find such a connection with another.
That's why I drink and smoke weed, to relieve the pressure of love... To lower my expectations on life.... To simplify my desires.... Maybe some wine and a vibrator is all I really need. And friends. I do have good friends who care about me. Problem is, they aren't in bed with me each night, holding me, kissing me, loving me, making me feel special and secure..... fuuuuck..... God? God? are you there? pleeeeez put this man in my life... I'm ready. I hate masturbating. I know it's selfish, I don't want to be selfish any more, I want a man I can give myself to, a man who can inspire me to step outside of myself... I don't care what color he is, God....he only has to be one color, God....yes you know what that color is, God, it's the color of Lo-

Oh shit, hell yeah, I just remembered I *do* have more batteries...

106

The Track

It had been four years since I'd seen Jack and I wasn't looking forward to seeing him that Friday afternoon. I suppose one shouldn't dislike their older brother for so long, that with age we should somehow look beyond our differences and appreciate the kinship. Whatever that means.

"Meet me at the old high school," he said over the phone. "One more race for old times' sake."

"Can't we just meet at a coffee shop, or grab a beer and burger somewhere? I haven't run in years." This was a lie because I ran every day, four miles a day, the final lap a full sprint.

"Oh quit your crying, Jimmy. Just meet me there. I have something I want to tell you."

"Are you gay?"

"Oh shut up, will ya?"

"Got a chic pregnant?"

"I wish," Jack sighed.

"Killed a man? Broke out of prison?"

"I'll see you Friday at noon, okay?"

"The test came back positive?"

He hung up.

It was weird talking to Jack that day. It had been four years since I'd seen him and almost a year since we'd talked. He left home in what my parents called a "drug addict's rage". He called it something else. Amid the profanities he mentioned something about escaping loveless oppression. I had no idea what he was talking about.

I arrived at the track at noon. There was no sign of Jack. It was a cool autumn day. A sweeping wind blew the leaves and their blended colors across the track, some sticking to the surrounding fence. I remember thinking that I should appreciate the beauty of these leaves before they shriveled up and disappeared, leaving the landscape winter barren. But beauty is something one feels and I felt nothing but a desire to be somewhere else. I'd rather have been meeting my friends for some beers, maybe smoking some grass; letting this Friday afternoon take me into another Friday evening of oblivion.

Waiting for Jack on a cold day at the same high school track he had once broke so many records was the sort of life experience I would much rather have avoided. Sometimes it's just easier to stick to one's life as it has become, not to be reminded too much of the past, to accept time's softening of hard questions about what is and what was until those questions eventually become more manageable murmurs in the less severe part of your mind.

I had been at the track for nearly ten minutes when I noticed a figure sitting on a bench at the opposite end. It appeared to be an old man, frail and slouched, protecting himself from the brisk breeze. This figure unnerved me. There was something about strangers in isolation, looking lonely and weak, that discomforted me.

As I watched him, this old man rose and began walking towards me, his feet dragging across the surface of the track with each step.

I scanned the surroundings for Jack. I felt strange all of a sudden, a feeling of vulnerability disrupting my sense of security. Who was this strange man? Why was he approaching me? I suddenly found myself begging a God I did not believe in to deliver Jack to me at that very moment. Jack with his powerful legs. Jack with his strong arms. Jack with his swollen chest.

I considered sprinting back to the car but nervously laughed off the notion. What was I afraid of? Another strong gust and this old man would fall down and break his bones.

I turned with my back to this feeble old man and scanned the empty parking lot. I watched my breath cloud before me and thought that maybe I should have smoked a joint before coming. Perhaps I was too tightly wound.

"You ready?" A voice surprised me.

I spun around, ready to confront the old man who'd crept up on me so quickly, but my startled eyes were alarmed to meet the fading familiarity of a weathered face and gray eyes that were not those of an old man at all.

"Jack? Is that you?"

"Yeah lil bro, who'd you think it was?"

"You look like shit," I said, scanning this perplexing vestige of my big brother.

"Nice to see you too," Jack said annoyed. "Damn. Haven't seen my little bro in four years and this is how I'm greeted."

"Sorry Jack, but damn, you looked like an old man from far away."

"And how do I look now?"

I couldn't answer him. He looked terrible. It was as if the meat of his face, the life of his face, had been removed and all that remained was pallid skin stretched thin upon sharp bone. His once vibrant green eyes were now gray and had fallen deep within two dark shadows of his skull.

"Nevermind me. Ready to race?" Jack said, taking off his coat.

"Race?" He couldn't have been serious. Race? Had he looked at himself lately?

"Yeah. It's been a while. One more race for old time's sake."

"You look like you can barely walk. How are you supposed to run?"

"Listen Jimmy, don't tell me what I can and cannot do. If you don't want to race, then fine, just admit it you little chicken shit. Maybe you can finally beat me for once." Jack stretched, more ceremoniously than with serious intent to loosen up. "But don't count on it," he added.

It was true I had never beaten him. Not once. Not even close. Jack was a phenomenally gifted runner; so gifted he was awarded a full scholarship to the University of Michigan. This scholarship and the dream opportunity it offered would only last until two weeks into the second semester of his freshmen year, at which time Jack abruptly quit the team. He left school a short time after.

"Are you actually talking shit?" I asked, only slightly stunned. "You look sick. Like the walking dead. And now you're talking shit? Are you out of your mind?"

"Just one more, Jimmy. Don't make this difficult. I need this."

He needed this. *He* needed this.

"How many laps?" I asked.

"Just one. Not sure I can do much more than that. A one lap sprint like when we were kids."

I ran hard and fast. Perhaps harder and faster than I had ever run. Jack was never close and I never looked back. When I crossed the finish line and the blur of my enraged adrenalin began to clear, I noticed Jack was smoking a cigarette in the middle of the track, only a few yards from the starting line. He was coughing and laughing.

I walked over.

"You finally did it, lil bro. You beat me. You beat Jack. How does it feel?"

I said nothing.

"You don't have to answer. I know it felt good."

"Are you a drug addict, Jack?"

"Not anymore."

"Are you dying?"

"Some might call it that. But that's not why I'm here. This isn't about me. This is about you, Jimmy."

It was strange, this moment. His eyes, dark and deep; his skin, pale and weathered; his voice, shaking but focused.

Jack took a drag off his cigarette, coughed wildly through the exhale, then glanced briefly up towards me.

"I've given you 26 years of nothing, lil bro," he said. "I could have been so many things to you, but instead I was nothing. Less than nothing."

"That's not true," I lied.

"It doesn't matter what you say. I know it's true."

"So are you dying?"

"Stop asking me that fucking question, goddamnit. This isn't about me. How many goddamned times do I have to say it?"

I asked the question but it was an empty question; a question to solve a mystery rather than to spark an emotion. I just wanted to know.

Jack looked up at me once more, then back down towards a fresh autumn leaf he was now holding in his cold and shaking hand. "I love you, Jimmy," he whispered weakly to the autumn leaf.

I said nothing. I wanted to leave.

"You don't have to say anything. Just know that, well...I really do love you. And I'm not who I once was. That's all."

The way Jack looked at me- I could tell he wanted me to comfort him, to say something that would assure him that he was being too hard on himself. I couldn't lie though. I couldn't sound convincing even if I did lie. So I said nothing.

No longer able to look towards my big brother, I gazed absently at the roughness of an autumn leaf that I had trapped beneath my foot.

Jack coughed, stroked the soft and colorful autumn leaf in his hand.

"Jimmy," he managed through increased coughing, "I don't want you to look like this one day." Jack's cough was heavy and deep and loud. "I don't want you to look like me. That's all."

This leaf beneath my foot was void of vibrant color. It was shriveled and brown. Dead. I wondered why I thought more about this leaf than I did what Jack was telling me.

"If you don't mind," Jack said with a whisper, his cough subsiding. "I think I'll return to that bench over there for a while. You go ahead and leave. Don't worry about me. Just know I love you. That's all."

I wanted to step on this dead leaf, to hear the crunch beneath my foot. A child's voice begged me to flatten its shriveled shape, to crush its cuplike reach that angled upwards towards me.

It may have been seconds. Perhaps minutes. Hell, it could have been an hour- I don't recall. But suddenly there came a long gust of sweeping wind that persisted for several moments. It was at the height of this wind that I chose to lift my foot and let that shriveled autumn leaf drag powerlessly across the track. It quickly disappeared into the indecipherable chaos of the infinite others.

I scanned my surroundings and noticed once again that strange old man, slouched and alone, sitting on a distant bench.

I rose to my feet and turned towards the parking lot, my back to this old man.

With fresh autumn leaves swirling like a nuisance in the wind and the dead ones crunching beneath my feet, my strides quickened.

What's Crazy

What's crazy is the possibility that someone you've offered so much truth would destroy you in the end.

Vanishing Faces

It was a night like many others.

"Hey baby, it's cool, okay? – you've had a lot in your system tonight."

Elliot stares deep into the back of the black leather seat, into the tiny holes, into his frustrated emotion, his inability to pretend.

"Hel*looo*? Are you okay?" Alexis asks, head tilted to the side, eyebrows arched.

Elliot rubs his temple slowly.

"I feel like I'm in a movie," he finally says.

"Which one?"

"A bad one."

"I'm not sure how I'm supposed to take that, so I won't."

Elliot fails to respond and silence dominates the mood.

It is raining. It's been raining for hours, a steady methodical drizzle.

"I like rain," Elliot finally says.

"Rain?"

"The sound. I like the sound of rain, the sounds rain creates."

"I like snow," Alexis offers.

"Snow is visual. Beautifully visual. Rain is for the ears. Soothing."

"Wet though."

Alexis looks at Elliot with a smile. He is staring blankly into the foggy window, drawing a circle with his pinky finger.

"Cleansing…glossy…peaceful…" he whispers.

"What about storms?" Alexis asks.

Elliot ignores her, retraces the circle he has drawn on the window.

"This feels nice," he says. "The cool whatever this foggy stuff is called against my finger."

"Condensation?"

"Condensation."

Elliot draws three more circles with his pinky, creating a triangle of circles.

Alexis rummages through her purse.

"Steady drizzles," Elliot says. "Storms are different. It's the drizzles I like. I like that word. Drizzle." Elliot closes his eyes as he says this, letting the sound of the rain consume him.

"Drizzle, drizzle, drizzle," Alexis says, breaking Elliot from his momentary trance. "Yeah, not a bad word. Z's are cool to say-zzzzzeeeee."

Elliot ignores Alexis as she continues to search through her purse. He re-traces his circles once more.

"Can you hear that?" he asks.

"What?"

"Shhhhhh, listen."

"You're weird."

Elliot raises his hand to Alexis' mouth to keep her from talking.

"It's musical," he says with little emotion. "Rain meeting car. Pat-Pat-Pat. Steady and soothing." Elliot taps the ceiling of the car to the beat. He stares at his fingers, wonders why they are shaking.

"You're weird," Alexis complains.

Elliot inhales deeply and exhales, "Fuck words."

Alexis finds what she is looking for in her purse. Bending forward, she places the purse on the front seat. Elliot watches her, her naked skin, her caramel colored, curvy backside. He rubs his penis for a second, stops, and looks away towards the vanishing circles.

Alexis rubs his cold thigh, he feels awkward. She speaks.

"Want some coke? The pills are dying, I mean mine are, are yours?"

Elliot retraces his first circle, adds eyes, a nose, and a crooked smile.

"I like being safe and sheltered and warm when it rains…cold rain…warm rain is different," Elliot says as if in a dream, or a nightmare.

Alexis opens the vial of coke and is concentrating hard not to spill any as she knocks a bump out on her hand.

Elliot quietly continues, "Is cold rain heavier? It feels it. A thicker beat, better sound than warm rain maybe."

Alexis snorts the coke, extends the vial towards Elliot.

"Want?" she asks.

Elliot takes the vial without looking while watching his crooked smiley face stare at him strangely.

"Storms?" He asks absently, then faintly smiles as he says "Thunder is threatening. Thunder and lightning *are* exciting though."

"I'm getting restless," Alexis groans impatiently.

Elliot retraces another circle, adds narrow eyes, a button nose, and a frown.

"But drizzle gets old and annoying and boring after a while," he concludes.

"And wet and muddy," Alexis offers.

Elliot retraces another vanishing circle, adds no face, crosses an X through the crooked smiley face.

"So we need thunder and lightning to appreciate the steady tap tap tapping of drizzle..." Elliot trails off.

"Drizzle drizzle drizzle..."

"-on the roof of your car."

"Elliot, are you still E-ing?"

Elliot unscrews the vial of cocaine. "The tapping is annoying me now," he complains.

"I'm restless," Alexis repeats.

Elliot dumps out a massive mound of coke on the side of his hand and sniffs and snorts and exhales loudly.

"Boom, Bam, Bang...Thunder is power...Boom, Crack, Bam!" he exclaims.

"Feeling better?" Alexis asks with a smile.

Elliot crosses out the frowny face, retraces the fourth circle, and adds big eyes, a small nose, and a very large smile. He looks at Alexis and smiles. She grabs his cool fingers and smiles back.

"May I lick your breasts, Alexis?"

"Why yes of course, Rainman."

They both laugh. Elliot gently massages Alexis' inner groin, teasingly brushing over her moist vagina. He grazes her neck and ears with kisses, moving his way down to her large, soft breasts, until he is nibbling on her left nipple, fingers inside of her. He feels something, she senses it, he pushes it against her cool thigh, she grabs the back of his head, kissing him hard on the mouth........the faces quickly vanish.

***

Elliot is holding Alexis, his right bicep loose against her right breast.

"You know the worst thing about losing yourself?" he asks.

"What?"

"You don't know it, you don't see it. I mean it just happens."

Alexis is stroking Elliot's right forearm with her middle finger, eyes closed.

"Dangerous," he says.

"Yeah, scary too."

"Very scary."

The two sit in silence for seconds that seem like minutes. Hearts are racing, legs are shaking, nerves are begging.

"It's like I think I'm positive I know what, who, or where I am on Friday, and then on Sunday I am thinking or acting, just *am* totally different, or like totally regretful of the other me's actions," Elliot says, annoyed by this self-revelation.

Alexis remains silent, eyes shut.

"Maybe I'm schizo. Are you asleep?"

"You're fucking human, Elliot," Alexis says.

"Is that supposed to make me feel better?"

"You think too much."

"That'll be the death of me."

"What?"

"Thinking."

"Yeah."

Elliot strokes Alexis' hair.

"What's up with the future?" Elliot asks rhetorically.

"The future?"

Elliot knocks out a line and snorts it loudly.

"What about the future, Elliot?"

Elliot draws a smiley face on the window.

"Ahhh nothing..."

"What do you mean?"

Elliot rubs out the face, clearing the window, and squints to look outside.

"Thunder baby, did you hear that?"

Alexis sits up.

"Come here Elliot. You need a hug."

They hug, a light hug with heavy chemical emotion.

"Would you like me to please you with my tongue?" Elliot asks, serious.

"I'd rather you hold me, to tell you the truth Elliot."

He squeezes her tighter.

"Hugs are nice."

"They're amazing."

They hold for seconds, not minutes, then separate. Alexis dumps out a small hill of coke on Elliot's thigh, leans down and snorts, then hands the vial to him and rests her head on Elliot's lap, closing her eyes and squeezing his hand gently.

"Alexis?"

"Yes Elliot?"

"Who do you blame?"

"For what?"

"This."

"You mean who do I thank?"

"For drugs?"

"No Elliot, for you, for this."

Elliot smiles sarcastically. Rolling his eyes, he knocks out a bump of coke and snorts.

"I'd like to take you somewhere nice, somewhere sober," he says, a new dose of ambition speeding through his veins.

"I'd like that," Alexis says with sincerity.

"Yeah."

Elliot squeezes her hand, she squeezes back. He lets go to wipe his running nose, leaving a red streak behind on the back of his hand. The drizzle has stopped. The car is getting cold. Alexis' eyes are open and she is staring. Elliot is also staring, curious of the time, noticing a light shade of blue slowly replacing the darkness outside the car. Someone is sweeping in front of a Sushi bar, a garbage truck roars by, an elderly man is jogging.

Elliot forces a yawn as he leans to the front of the car and turns up the stereo.

"Maybe this is as good as it gets," Alexis says, sniffling

"What time is it?" Elliot asks, blowing red snot into a white napkin.

"Time to finish this coke."

"Yeah, good answer."

"Yeah."

One Hour before the Veil of Vesuvius

One hour before the veil of Vesuvius a young man was falling in love with the girl down the way in the yellow house, the one with the dimples and soft hands.
One hour before the veil of Vesuvius a warrior was beating his princess.
One hour before the veil of Vesuvius an elderly man with a rounded belly of wine tripped on a stone and fell to the ground and laughed at the state of his folly.
One hour before the veil of Vesuvius three red haired women slightly overweight and blatantly intoxicated lounged in a fresh water bath and laughed and drank wine and swapped jokes and perversions as candles flickered in a circle around them.
One hour before the veil of Vesuvius a young girl, unbathed and melancholy sat on her floor with legs crossed and hands gripping her sandy brown hair and allowed her sorrow to slide from her glossy green eyes and roll over her red round cheek bones and drip off her chin and no one will ever know why.
One hour before the veil of Vesuvius a black dog laid curled in a ball cooled in the shade of a lemon tree slightly snoring and dreamed of slow-footed rabbits.
One hour before the veil of Vesuvius a thirteen year old boy was found masturbating in the toilet and his petrified mother pointed her finger and frowned her face and punished him for weeks.
One hour before the veil of Vesuvius two lovers, one too young and one too old, made true love and promised lifelong devotion.
One hour before the veil of Vesuvius an elderly shopkeeper helplessly watched her shop as well as her home burn to the hard ground as young boys on their way home from school scurried back and forth from well to fire, with buckets of water but this helped none and the dejected shopkeeper could foresee no comfort in the future.
One hour before the veil of Vesuvius a girl of five wandered the uneven streets in search of her gray cat with the black spot covering the right paw and experienced discomfort in the face of a fat drunk man sprawled against the curb swigging his wine and sticking his tongue out at her.
One hour before the veil of Vesuvius the wife of the lazy bald man with the scar on his right temple cooked her husband a plate of pasta and let it

sit on the table even though he was an hour late and sometimes never returned home and was rumored by the three fat red-haired ladies to have a mistress maybe two.

One hour before the veil of Vesuvius a man of maybe twenty licked the left breast of the Brothel Princess and was eager to skip foreplay so he could get the pleasure out of money without much thought and without much time.

One hour before the veil of Vesuvius a young girl beautiful and wealthy experienced guilt at the sight of a blind beggar but then refused to believe he was really blind and went home and felt her breasts in the mirror and lit a candle and drank some red wine and fiddled with her gold jewelry and drank some more red wine and was bored but a little drunk and horny and went to one of her boyfriends' houses and had sex.

One hour before the veil of Vesuvius a bearded man lied to his lover and laughed about it over a bottle of whiskey he shared with his single friend.

One hour before the veil of Vesuvius a wife who had lied to her husband was found in bed with another woman and her husband exploded into a maniacal laugh before strangling them both and returning to the pub.

One hour before the veil of Vesuvius a boy lied to his mother.

One hour before the veil of Vesuvius a mother lied to her daughter.

One hour before the veil of Vesuvius a tired servant laid down for a quick nap on his master's bed and had a vivid dream about pulling a bottle of wine from a golden bucket and pouring a glass for his master's naked wife and she was laughing and he was confident and she said she loved him and he kissed her and then he woke up to find her yelling at him and looking haggard and he fetched more firewood.

One hour before the veil of Vesuvius Apollo was being revered and no one was asking why.

One hour before the veil of Vesuvius a breeze rustled leaves and birds chirped out of tune and a group of young children screeched and giggled.

One hour before the veil of Vesuvius an orange was peeled by dirty fingers.

One hour before the veil of Vesuvius a tired and sweaty craftsman took a swig from a jug of water and wiped sweaty sawdust from his forehead and water from his chin and squinted into the sky and let out a magnificent yawn while stretching his muscular arms in a V and thought about something that made him smile.

One hour before the veil of Vesuvius a young girl lost her virginity and wondered what the big deal was as her dark lover slept.

One hour before the veil of Vesuvius three drunk bricklayers on break whistled a surprisingly enchanting melody with their eyes closed as an orange kitten sat beneath a shrub and eyed them suspiciously.

One hour before the veil of Vesuvius a pale-skinned boy farted in class and blushed bright red as his classmates pointed fingers and plugged their noses and made simulated fart noises of their own.

One hour before the veil of Vesuvius a long-haired poet with a pointy chin and crater skin sat alone drinking cheap red wine trying to describe or justify or give meaning to his existence or of that around him but tried even harder to resist the temptation of the Brothel.

One hour before the veil of Vesuvius a whore became content and her customers richer.

One hour before the veil of Vesuvius a black-haired red faced painter half smiled a crooked smile as he detailed the beautiful mountain in the distance that crept mysteriously through a colony of clouds resembling an apple a foot a face and into the ocean blue sky.

One hour before the veil of Vesuvius a black haired man with a bushy black mustache and droopy black eyes drove his chariot the wrong way down a one way street despite the posted sign and a woman wearing a black dress and carrying some pottery yelled in a screechy voice something about the man's intoxication.

One hour before the veil of Vesuvius a boy carved the name Lucius into the side of his cousin's shop wall with a stone he proudly sharpened the night previous.

One hour before the veil of Vesuvius a Mother washed the wavy flowing red hair of her only child and the child felt loved and the Mother felt loving as the sun beamed through the window creating a square shaped sun spot on the chest of the child.

One hour before the veil of Vesuvius a single man named Antonio walked slowly away from the sun staring at his bouncing shadow that looked limp and lifeless with sagging shoulders and dragging feet and couldn't remember why he was doing it but knew he must and he couldn't stop staring as his shadow paused at its destination and he mumbled something in a low whisper before jumping off a cobblestone bridge towards what he vowed was a new beginning.

One hour before the veil of Vesuvius a young woman gave birth to a healthy baby that didn't even cry and gazed out her window with newborn in her arms and was serenely amazed at how simple and clear and pure life could be.

One hour before the veil of Vesuvius the temperature of a presumptuous existence began to rise.

Dull Pressure Strangulation

I am stabbing my father in the throat. It feels good. But his fingers are on my throat and he won't let go. He is strangling me with a soft force. His grip is not the brute force of fingers gripping violently the soft flesh of a neck. His fingers are only barely touching the skin. The contact is minimal. I have stabbed him now 20 or 30 times in the face and throat, and with each stab the pressure of his grip has weakened, but the effect of his grip has continued to increase in severity. How is this so when the actual hold he has over me has diminished to a faint touch? How is it that the lightest touch of his fingers upon my neck now makes breathing impossible? Why won't he just let go? Why won't he give up? I stab him several more times in rapid succession and his grip becomes nothing more than a dull physical sensation, yet the strangulation I am suffering has grown more severe. I can't explain it. I suddenly cease my stabbing because I feel my arms are succumbing to a rapid onset of paralysis. I cannot breathe. I am unable to move. Why won't he just die? Everything about my father has become lifeless except his eyes and the soft fingers that are constricting the muscles in my neck with dull pressured force. I want to plead with him, to tell him I'm sorry, to beg for his release. But I cannot. My rage has flamed out and only fear remains as I look into his bloodshot, vacant eyes. I try to shake myself free but paralysis has now spread throughout my body, the only exception being the toes on my right foot. I move these toes with a wild desperation, hoping they will somehow spark the rest of my body to regain control and movement. How is it that only my toes, these tiny limbs furthest from my brain, are still free to move? The room becomes dark and I am being taken unwillingly to some sort of black hole, a mysterious place of inevitable cruelty, and I am being pulled there by the powers of my powerlessness and my father's unwillingness to die.

Suburban Samaritan

The body laid twisted and dying in the roadside ditch.

The beats and lyrics of Tupac reverberated through the deserted highway night.

The early hour sky was dark and heavy.

The exhaust pipe breathed dense clouds of smoke into the late night air, the continuous exhale illuminated by the red glow of taillights.

Swaying from heal to toe, toe to heal, Tim admired the line of urine shooting from his soft, numb penis. His nose was running and his mouth still tasted like Jaeger shots.

Tim was searching for his pack of cigarettes in his coat when he heard an awful moan sound from the darkness beyond the road.

He pissed on his shoe and his hand and down his leg as he back-pedalled quickly away from the sound and towards the car. He shoved his soft small cold penis back into his jeans and scanned the blind blackness where the moan had sounded.

"What the fuck was that?" Tim whispered to himself. "Probably nothing," he hoped. "I'm just tweaking," he reasoned. "I'm way too fucked up," he concluded.

Tim reached deep into the pocket of his jeans and removed an orange vial. He unscrewed its black cap, turned it on its side, and tapped a large white mound onto his left hand. He then quickly sucked the powder up his nose and let out a satisfactory grunt as his senses quickly returned to more desirable heights and his thoughts and perceptions instantly moved in the opposite direction of fear.

"Gotta be a stupid fucking animal," he laughed. "Probably a deer. The bastard is probably dying."

Tupac's "California Love" screamed loudly from the car as Tim inhaled another large mound of white. He bounced his hand in the air and altered his fingers to resemble a gang sign. Tim then lit a cigarette, took a drag, and exhaled. With a loud declaration, as if speaking directly to Tupac, Tim screamed: "YEAH MY NIIIIIIIGGEEEEERRRRR.....YEEEEEAAAAA MOTHERFUCKER.....YOU MY NIGGER FOR LIFE, PAC......YEEAAA".

Tim's friends in the car each rapped along.

When the song ended, Tim's friends prepared for themselves another round of snort and cough and smile. The silence of the early morning returned and Tim scanned the darkness, ready to venture into the black unknown and confirm for certain the stupidity of his previous fear.

As he began his walk towards the edge of the road, he heard the sound of movement over dead leaves and then another moan, this one much louder and sustained. Tim paused in his tracks, his eyes wide towards darkness before him.

He quickly tapped another white mound on the back of his hand, this one much larger than the others, and consumed it. He continued his walk into the blackness of the night, towards this haunting moan.

Standing at the edge of the embankment, Tim found himself looking at the barely visible outline of what appeared to be a body. Dropping to one knee, he lit his lighter and extended its weak illumination forward until this shape below became more visible. There was no question it was a body. It was the body of a woman; a dark woman with thin black braids and large black eyes. She was barely clothed and her body was twisted among the dead leaves and roadside trash. Her face was swollen and one of her legs looked broken. Blood soaked part of her white dress and there appeared to be blood on her face and neck as well.

Upon seeing Tim, she moaned once more, this time softer, as if pleading for Tim's help. Tim sat motionless for several moments as he watched this tangled and battered body.

A voice suddenly shouted from the car, breaking Tim out of his stunned trance.

"What the fuck is it, Tim?"

Tim did not respond. He wasn't sure how to respond.

"Yo, are you fucking deaf?" A friend asked with irritation. "What the fuck are you looking at?"

Tim rose to his feet, took a long drag from his cigarette, and walked slowly back to the car. "It's a fucking body," he said, leaning inside the passenger side window.

"What did you say?" A voice shouted from the backseat.

"Did you say *body*?" The other voice from the backseat said.

Tupac was lowered on the stereo a couple notches.

"Yeah," Tim said.

"A dead body? A human dead body? Or an animal?" Tim's friend in the passenger seat asked as he stuck a rolled up dollar bill into his nose, lowered his head, and inhaled a large line from the mirror in his hand.

"Hook me up with that shit," Tim said.

"Is the body dead, Tim? Is it an animal or a human?"

"Just lift that fucking mirror to my face and hand me that dollar bill. I need to get my head straight on this shit."

Tim inhaled three of the remaining five lines and coughed into the night as the surge moved through him.

"What the fuck, man?!"

"You were only supposed to take one!"

"Are you trying to give yourself a goddamn heart attack? Jesus fucking Christ."

A wild charge of hyper euphoria spread through Tim and he began jumping up and down and rolling his shoulders.

"Oh quit your fucking crying and turn Tupac back up," Tim said with amused arrogance.

"I'm not turning shit up until you tell me about that body," the friend in the front seat said.

"Why don't you go look for your own fucking self," Tim laughed. "Is someone going to role a joint?" Tim reached into the car and turned up the stereo. "That's my nigger right there," Tim said, then began rapping with the song.

"I'm definitely checking out that supposed fucking body," Tim's front seat friend said. "As soon as I take another blast."

The Tupac song ended and in the silence between tracks, the moan returned, this time much louder and haunting. The others didn't hear it, but Tim did.

Wiping the numbing wetness from his nose, Tim knew he must help this woman. He fully intended on doing so. He just hadn't determined how. It was complicated. She was really messed up. And so was he. Surely the police would suspect Tim of being high and drunk. There was no concealing it. Surely it would be protocol to search Tim and his friends and even search Tim's car considering how serious this woman was messed up. Tim considered putting her in his car and dropping her at the hospital, but she didn't even look like she could be moved. What if he hurt her even more? What if he suddenly became incriminated?

Inside the car Tim could hear the sound of someone sucking snot up his nose. Tupac lyrics were once again being recited. Laughter was rising.

"You know it's pretty fucking stupid to sit here on the side of the road, seeing that we're probably committing like fifty fuckin felonies," a backseat friend barked as more sniffing was followed by coughing and grunting. The volume on the stereo was suddenly cranked up and all the friends in the car started rapping along to TuPac, laughing and howling like maniacs.

Tim began pacing back and forth, wondering what he could and would do. His nose was running and his teeth were grinding.

"Ok," the front seat friend said. "Let's check this *body* out. If's that's really what it is." Tim was relieved he would be able to share the burden of this dilemma with another.

As the front seat friend began to step out of the car, a pair of headlights suddenly illuminated the early morning sky.

"Shit! Someone's coming over the hill!" A friend screamed.

"Fuck! Tell those assholes to turn the music down and hide that shit!" Tim said to his front seat friend.

Tim walked rapidly back and forth, trying to determine some course of action to take if this was a cop.

"Pretend you're fixing your tire," the front seat friend said.

"I don't even know how to do that," Tim said.

"Who fucking cares! Just fake it!"

The approaching car reached the peak of the hill and began descending towards Tim and his friends. Tim ran around the car and squatted beside the roadside front tire. His legs were shaking. So were his hands. It was the cold air. It was the possibility of getting arrested. It was those three monster lines he had just inhaled.

Tim grabbed the inner part of the hubcap to keep his balance. "Motherfucker," Tim said to himself. Thoughts of getting arrested drunk and with drugs while driving his old man's Mercedes incited a new kind of surge inside of Tim. Fear combined with the drugs made Tim shiver wildly in the cold night.

The approaching car was less than fifty yards away and began to slow. Tim began fiddling with the wheel- sticking his fingers into the hubcap and weakly pressing the hard rubber tire with his bony fingers.

The approaching car veered slowly into the right lane and rolled closer. Tim expected at any moment to see flashing police lights strobe into the night sky. To face an officer's flashlight shining in his eyes. To feel the cold steel of handcuffs on his wrists.

Tim felt dizzy and weak. He wondered if such an arrest would be reported to the entrance board and lead to the rejection of his recent acceptance.

The approaching car, whose shape and color was concealed by its high beams, crept nearer to Tim at an increasingly slow pace. Tim's squatting became awkward and unstable as his anxiety rose and he felt his weight pulling him backwards, towards the street. To sustain his position, Tim reached his shaky hands towards the inner curve of the tire. He needed a firmer grip. But in doing so, his hands slipped off the tire completely and he fell back hard onto the black asphalt. As Tim frantically tried to collect himself, the car pulled next to him.

Tim did not look at the car as he rose to his knees and nervously poked and pulled at the hubcap. He heard a window roll down and music playing softly. Tim could feel the heat from inside the car blanket the back of his neck.

"Hey man, are you OK? Do you need some help?" The voice in the car asked. Tim turned around and leaned his back against the tire. The man in the car had dark brown skin and a round nose. His eyes were narrow and kind.

"No, i-it's cool. My hubcap fell off, that's all," Tim managed.

The dark brown man in the car glanced briefly at Tim's three wide-eyed friends who sat tense in Tim's car, looking suspicious and wired. He then returned his puzzled expression back to Tim and said, "You look a little sick, why don't you let those guys handle it?"

Tim forced a small chuckle and assured the kind man that it was okay, that he was "just a bit tired, that's all."

Tim felt his face twitch, his hands shake, and his nose drip. His eyes were wide, his pupils full.

The man looked perplexed, but said, "Alright, just thought I'd make sure you were okay. I've got a phone in here if you need to use it." The man lifted his cell phone to offer as proof.

Tim rubbed his nose and forced a smiled.

"No, that's okay, thanks anyway though. I got one in the car."

The man then put his car into drive and said, "OK, well good luck to you boys, take care." He waved as he drove off and Tim and his friends all waved back.

Suddenly a roar of laughter erupted from the car. They were all laughing at Tim.

Tim quickly jumped into the car and drove off.

"What'd the fancy nigger want?" A backseat friend laughed.

"Probably thought little white boy Timmy here was cute," another backseat friend retorted.

Tim quickly switched the CDs, replacing TuPac with Dave Matthews as he continued to accelerate.

"What about that body?" The front seat friend asked.

"Fuck it," Tim said.

This response was met with laughter but Tim was not laughing.

Hope

Frozen
Out of focus
Exhausted
Stability lost
Trapped
Shaking
Misery churns
Slow motion
Confidence shrinking
Each submission.
Weak fucking mystery
Shudders in the morning
Numbed by evening
Temporarily drowned at
Midnight.
Dance unsure
Sanity blurs
Further
Further into the
Fake-ass kingdom
Cosmetic wealth
Driven by moods
Possessed by
Demons fed by
The chemical nutrients
We so dutifully
Provide.
Scared to live pure
Terrified to maintain strength
The newspaper depresses
Hollywood strokes
Alcohol releases
Mornings plague.
Play pretend
Attain the greatest tan

Dress dying flesh with
Flashy threads
Drunkenly declare
The noble cause
The "if only" speech
The different approach
Just wait and see...
Tortured battle to be real
To live free
To fully attain
The dreamy clear purity
Contentment
That is the true destiny
But
Reality
Hazes and
Delivers
Shade drawn days
Deer Hunter nights.
Yes it's true...
Full of shit!
Shit that combusts with truth like
Gas with Fire.
Will to live has
Yet to die
But
Good Days
Bad Weeks
Good Days
Bad Weeks
Repeat
Repeat
A beg a plea a
Miracle...
Maybe.
Flirt
One day
Strangle
The next.
Net yet stuffed
Stiff in a box
Kept alive by...

Kill My Dealer

The opposite of high is hell. And after a while, high becomes low and hell becomes hotter. I'm burning up.

I've got to kill my dealer. I've got to kill my father. I've got to kill my girlfriend and all my friends. I've got to kill my boss and my boss's boss. I've got to kill my mother and my older brother. I've got to kill the past, the present and the future.

The Red Neon Sign

"I can't concentrate."

"On what?"

"I can't concentrate on anything. It's weird."

"Then don't."

"Don't concentrate on anything?"

"Correct. Why does being able to concentrate hold such importance with you?"

"Because it...well... doesn't one need to be able to concentrate in order to achieve?"

"What are you trying to achieve?"

"Knowledge. Knowledge seems to be the root of all achievement."

"Why do you want to achieve something so fickle?"

"Because knowledge sets us free."

"Now that is embarrassingly cliché, is it not?"

"Just because it is cliché does not mean it is less true."

"What exactly does it set us free from?"

"Well that's a loaded question if I ever heard one."

"You made the statement, so is it not fair to ask you to back that statement up with some degree of substance?"

"Knowledge empowers us. Without knowledge, we are..."

"Yes?"

"Oh, I don't know. I am not that deep. I just know, as does anyone with half a brain, that knowledge is necessary in life if we are to possess any sort of power. And quite simply, without power we are powerless. Nobody wants to be powerless."

"What sort of power are you speaking of? Power over what?"

"Others, I suppose. And ourselves."

"Okay, there you go making generalized, clichéd statements again. Lets go back to this knowledge thing. What kind of knowledge are you referring to? How does one achieve such an all encompassing goal? Surely you are referring to a specific sort of knowledge. What sort of knowledge are aiming for?"

"Oh I don't know. A wide array of knowledge. What? What is with that face?"

"You are impossible. How are you supposed to attain something if you can't even begin to define it? That's like saying your mission in life is to go to a place but you haven't a clue as to what that place is."

"I'm sorry you feel that way."

"Even if you were to specify a certain kind of knowledge, how do you even know what you will know will even be true? Knowledge must be acquired. How do you know the source of acquisition isn't corrupt?"

"I don't, I suppose."

"So you are going to devote your life to something that may not even be as it seems to be? Seems like an awfully pointless endeavor to me."

"I'm not sure I follow."

"Oh don't be so naïve. People read history books and news articles and biographies and self help guides and the Bible and whatever other source they can get their hands on to feel some sense of control over something that is in perpetual motion, always evolving, never predictable, masterfully deceitful: Life. It is quite the comical scene if you ask me."

"I think you are over-complicating things."

"Have you yet thought of at least a general category of knowledge you'd like to so nobly pursue?"

"I am not sure. This concentration thing is making that determination quite difficult. I feel doomed from the start. I suppose I should make a list and prioritize as to what I most want to know first."

"How funny you are! Make a list and prioritize! People are so tragic! To live one's life making lists and prioritizing must be a riveting existence! Ha ha ha h ah ha ha h!!"

"Okay Mr Sarcastic, what would you suggest?"

"Go ahead, start your list. This should be interesting."

"I will. Despite your facetiousness. Well... I've always wished I knew more about politics. I vote at almost every election without ever doing the proper research, without feeling confident I am making the right decision."

"Now there is a pointless endeavor if I've ever heard one."

"Can I finish?"

"By all means..."

"The history of Africa. More about the Civil Rights movement, including Malcolm X and the Black Panther Movement. And I'd like to know how to fix a car. That would save me a lot of money. And poetry-I'd like to learn the mechanics of how to write good poems?"

"Mechanics of poetry?"

"Yes."

"Mechanical poetry?"

"What?"

"Isn't that a contradiction in itself?"

"No, I mean the basics of poetry, like-"

"Basic poetry? How boring."

"Oh forget it. This is an idiotic conversation. I do not have to rationalize my desire to have knowledge. Only a fool would not aspire towards knowledge."

"But you've already confessed your inability to concentrate. So perhaps you are destined to be a fool."

"Maybe knowledge can be attained without concentration."

"How so?"

"Well...let me think for a moment... I got it: through experience. One does not have to be a scholar to attain knowledge. Knowledge can be achieved through experience alone. There have been plenty of very wise, very knowledgeable people who could not read or write. They simply experienced."

"So how are you going to experience the Civil Rights era and the Black Panther party? How are you going to experience the history of Africa? How are you going to experience the issues in a political election? Watch the campaign commercials? Ha!"

"I don't know."

"May I make an observation?"

"No."

"Well, I will anyway. I think you are so hung up on achieving this phantom thing called knowledge because you think it will make you feel less insignificant. Maybe you need to find significance in something else – something less grand and idealistic."

"Like what?"

"I don't know. Whatever it is, it mustn't require concentration."

"What significant achievements in life don't require concentration?"

"Those that require little thinking."

"I see. And what requires little thinking?"

"Pleasure, for one."

"What kind of pleasure?"

"Not the intellectual sort. That is not in the cards for you. The sort that is more base, more aligned perhaps with the basics of human nature."

"Can seeking pleasure for one's self really be counted as an achievement?"

"Is not achievement by its very nature an act of pleasure? Do we not achieve because it brings us a special sort of pleasure? Don't let life's noblest of people fool you – their noble acts first and foremost bring them pleasure."

"I suppose you are correct."

"I know I am correct. So if we have identified that everything in the end comes down to pleasing one's self, then we must define alternate forms of pleasure, or avenues of pleasure that are more realistic for the individual that is you. And knowledge, I am sorry to say, is not in the cards. Knowledge is a lot of work. It requires reading. Listening. Remembering. *Experiencing*. These are laborious exercises that require attentiveness and concentration. Having pointed out that you lack these things, I think it is best you quit torturing your poor self and quit this fantasy land of knowledge for a more realistic world of pleasure seeking."

"Tell me more. While you may be on to something, I am still skeptical."

"Yes, I know. Lets start listing off those things that bring you pleasure."

"Where do I start?"

"Anywhere. Whatever comes to your mind."

"Coffee."

"Boring. Devoting your life to coffee offers no promise. Keep thinking."

"Warm days"

"Warm days?"

"Yes. I love warm days either in the spring or in the fall or even in the middle of the winter when one of those unseasonably warm days arrive."

"Are you really this boring? I have asked you to name your greatest pleasures and all you could come up with was coffee and warm days. Are you a human being? Do you not crave a deeper sort of pleasure than these?"

"Deeper sort of pleasure, eh? Hmmm..."

"Drugs? Do you take drugs?"

"No. Not since I was in my twenties."

"Did you like them?"

"Naaah. There were some decent moments, but overall it was all a bit of a silly endeavor."

"Okay, what about women?"

"Well of course. I love women."

"Are you single?"

"No. I am married."

"Are you happy?"

"Yes. My wife is fantastic. Beautiful, smart, funny, loving…everything I could ask for."

"What do you miss most about before you were married?"

"I don't know. Nothing really."

"Marriage brings sacrifice. A man must give up certain things when he marries. Are you saying that there is nothing you have given up that you miss?"

"Well there is the obvious, of course."

"Sex? Women? Different women who bring the stimulation of new experiences? Love? Are these are the things you miss?"

"At times. But those things are nothing more than self centered, short sighted pursuits. Besides, who are we kidding? I am not a rock star. Look at this thinning hairline. Have you seen how tall I am? And I'm at least 30 pounds over weight. And my age. I'm almost 46 years old. That sort of life you are speaking of has passed me by. And whose to say I would enjoy true satisfaction from such a lifestyle? The love my wife and I share is something most men would die for."

"Are you bored?"

"With what?"

"The same woman. The same naked body."

"Not bored so much, but…"

"You are curious about what else it out there."

"Yes. There are so many beautiful women out there."

"Now we're on to something."

"Not really. Chasing a constant rotation of fresh female bodies seems to be a shallow sort of existence."

"Are you becoming more or less curious as time goes on?"

"I don't know."

"Sure you do."

"Ok, more, I suppose."

"Because you have nothing new and exciting to look forward to? It's all become predictable? Repetitive? Dull?"

"It can be. But I like it that way. Boring and predictable brings stability."

"You sound like a man constricted by fear. Is that why you married? You were scared of being alone?"

"I am sure that is a big reason most people marry. No one wants to be alone. And if you find someone you love and you marry that person, then you don't have to be alone. Was that the reason I got married? Absolutely not."

"We are always alone. Even when we are married."

"Now that's a cynical statement if I ever heard one."

134

"To pay attention to reality, is to sometimes be a cynic. That just comes with being perceptive and honest."

"So what is your point? Where is this conversation heading?"

"You need to experience new women, that is where I am going. You need to overcome this fear of being alone and you need to experience the warm body of a strange female who invites you to make love to her. Only then will you forgo this silly pursuit of knowledge. You need to experience pleasure in its most pure form. You need to make love to new and strange and exciting women."

"That is your conclusion? You think that will satisfy my thirst for knowledge?"

"It will satisfy another thirst. A thirst that is far more important. A thirst that when quenched will breathe a new life into you. It will make you feel less insignificant and less hung up on pursuits towards building self esteem and reassurances of purpose. Quenching this thirst will satisfy your most intense and needy and base need for pleasure."

"So that's it? That's your grand conclusion?"

"Yes, that is it. Let's be realistic: even with knowledge you are doomed. Knowledge does not bring that feeling of sex with a new woman. Knowledge does not bring the narcotic-like energy of a crush on a woman. Knowledge is a secondary pleasure, a much more dull and boring pleasure when compared to these other things. Perhaps that is why you can't concentrate on knowledge. It is more of a resignation. A distraction from the reality that you are a boring individual lacking stimulation. You figure you can't be dumb *and* bored- that has to be the worst state of all. So you try to read. You try to learn so you can impress others and yourself with your knowledge. This brings you a dim light of satisfaction, but it will never be a bright chandelier bursting with light. You have come to accept this dim light because it is far better than total darkness. But you don't have to live in the dull and dim light. You can charge that massive chandelier."

"So what is your conclusion? What should I do? Go have sex with a hooker?"

"I can not answer that question for you. I can only help to illuminate. Your actions are entirely up to you. Although I would have to say a hooker should probably be your last resort. A hooker is a resignation in itself. Unless you are one of those guys who experience deep emotional crushes for hookers, a guy who falls in love with hookers and believes them when they tell you between the metered time of 3:38AM and 4:28AM that they love you to, that you are the one, that you fuck better than any man in the universe. Shit, if you are one of those guys, then you've got it made. You can experience the whole package of emotional narcotics any night of the week. I am making the assumption you are not one of those guys. I am making the assumption that for you to burst that chandelier with blinding light, then the relationship you have with a new woman will have to be something less transactional, so to speak."

Ted no longer wishes to listen to his companion speak about what sort of pleasure he should be seeking. He rises from the brown table, a table layered with carvings wildly etched into its aged wood, and he puts his coat on. He finishes his beer and walks toward the crooked door, away from the dark and hazy booth, away from his strange companion.

"One more thing," Ted hears his companion say as he nears the door. "You must ask yourself whether it is self neglect or self preservation."

Ted swings open the door and a rush of cold air sweeps across his face. He has no idea what these words mean. And he has no desire to contemplate them. The door slams behind him.

Ted is standing beneath a red neon sign that hangs precariously above. He pulls his cell phone out of his pocket and eyes the first name in his phone directory:

Home

Ted circles the green "Send" button with the light pressure of his thumb. He looks above at the precarious red sign, noticing it for the first time. He glances back at the heavy wood door and its smoky window.

With a heavy breath, Ted slips his cell phone into his coat pocket and steps forward into the chaos of the night.

Chicago

1
Mad visions twisted with emotions
Are thrusting from their slumber
Begging to move south not north
With the calm of another ancient shovel of sauce
2
My ears burst into muffled silence
As I whisk to the crest, into the
Rustic heart of a man-mixed sky:
A bubbling stew seasoned with
Secrets
3
I drop a blemished 1977 quarter
Into the deceptive Spy Machine
And begin the dangerous exploration
Of humbling poetic scrutiny.
4
Zoom…Zoom…Zoom…
5
A deflated snowy-haired black man
Once marching behind Martin Jr.,
Many bottles previous
Is securely passed out in Grant Park
As the remains of his loyal obedient
Friend J.D. snakes its way toward a
Beautifully cultivated garden
Of blue, white, and red flowers.
6
A Streetwise vendor cradles her tender child
Two smiles radiating denial
Bouncing their way to the Ice Cream Parlor.
The stock market was up, the traders got higher
And the homeless got paid.
7
A corpulent Mexican lassie
Sits dejected on a crumbling curb

With the spine of a yellow hydrant
(What an awkward bone).
Her loneliness strums a modest melody
Unheard by the cheese-chasing rats scurrying past.
            8
A neon sign exclaiming:
"GUNS WE BUY AND SELL"
Shimmers in the face
Of a black-eyed boy.
His bitch of a mother just
Lost her job.
            9
An ex-girlfriend of mine
With the bod of a porn star
Goes mad on mushrooms
And I silently beg her to jump off
Her 31st floor balcony
So I can watch her crash through the roof
Of Planet Hollywood.
            10
A white bearded general
Reeking of tasty spirits barracho
Resembling the Hollywood Moses
Plays his harmonica out of tune
To a lonely white widow
And her 10 cent donation.
She has uncovered lucidity in his wayward blues.
            11
Oh yes, a missionary whore
Glides eloquently across the North Ave Bridge
And a 13 year old boy peddles quickly home
With her sermon still fresh in his groin.
            12
An obese women unpleasant to catwalk eye.
            13
Jovial juices mix with the blood
In her vein, bringing immediate
Warmth and meaning
To her dark-skinned day.
Her mind's at better use, her beauty now shines,
And she ponders phoning home
While the metropolis of her being floats unpolluted.

14
A half-eaten cheeseburger plummets
To the oil-stained crosswalk
As the yellow screaming blur freeze frames
Dead
And half a faceless cane lands silently in the grass.
15
Filthy bills line the chest of Commander Rafferty's
Bullet proof vest.
He is the Champion of Whiskey
And Pete, his son, my friend, I think,
Is hysterically high on C.
16
Abercrombie meatheads high on weights
And daddy's sheltered education sip Heineken
To the cry of B.B.
Under the plastic roof of the House of Blues.
They are incapable of feeling a darker people's
Genuine pain and fear and suffering and alienation,
But the music is catchy and the booze flows smooth.
17
Gunshots drown out giggles.
18
Sirens blare in the mysterious distance.
19
A poet's simplistic words mould simplistic poetry
In a tangled city
Self-concerned and conceited
Damned and applauded
Outright and secretive.
Deranged secrets are only revealed by mislead maniacs.
20
A death dealing nativity
The Windy City
The illuminated tragedy shining forth with its
Hot oily crimson powered energy
The Windy City
An interwoven sooty-segregation
Of tunnel-vision lunatics
The Windy City
21
And here I stand atop its Mecca

A sobering yawn my only movement
Stuck in the meaningless middle
Playing the role of a spectator poet
Without real purpose without real wisdom
Just cursed with these two hazel eyes
Twenty-one years of a beating heart
Doomed to see it all before
Being lured back down
To another dark swallow and hot burn and dulled ambition
With only one certainly awaiting my descent
The End

Distract Me til I...

He strolled forth through the hustle of the city.

The scene was rather typical for a city. Lots of different people. Lots of separate people. Lots of silently obsessing people.

He smiled at a recent revelation.

Some beers and just a little marijuana delivered the freedom of thought that fostered this revelation.

It had been a typical week of a hard and losing bargaining with life. The tightness of frustration had held permanent in his mind and in his body.

But those beers. That little marijuana. That revelation.

He continued to stroll through the city. Free. With a sense of purpose. A sense of knowing. Understanding.

He replayed this revelation over and over and over again in his mind.

Distract me til I die, he thought. *Distract me til I die.*

DISTRACT ME TIL I...

If you feel compelled to send me a note upon the conclusion of this collection, I would appreciate it.
Feedback of any variety is constructive feedback.
Your words are the winds that propel.

Thank you for diving into my creation…

J Merritt Lyons
therunningtap.com

jlmerritt@therunningtap.com

DISTRACT ME TIL I...

7775908R0

Made in the USA
Lexington, KY
13 December 2010